P9-CLA-895

This book is a work of fiction. Names, characters, places, and incidents are the
product of the author's imagination or are used fictitiously. Any resemblance to actual
events, locales, or persons, living or dead, is coincidental.

© 2018 MARVEL
Cover design by Ching Chan.

Hachette Book Group supports the right to free expression and the value of
copyright. The purpose of copyright is to encourage writers and artists to produce the
creative works that enrich our culture.

The scanning, uploading, and distribution of this book without permission
is a theft of the author's intellectual property. If you would like permission to
use material from the book (other than for review purposes), please contact
permissions@hbgusa.com. Thank you for your support of the author's rights.

Little, Brown and Company
Hachette Book Group
1290 Avenue of the Americas, New York, NY 10104
Visit us at LBYR.com

First Edition: June 2018

Little, Brown and Company is a division of Hachette Book Group, Inc.
The Little, Brown name and logo are trademarks of Hachette Book Group, Inc.

The publisher is not responsible for websites (or their content) that are not owned by
the publisher.

Library of Congress Control Number 2018936310

ISBNs: 978-0-316-48048-2 (pbk.); 978-0-316-48050-5 (ebook)

Printed in the United States of America

LSC-C

10 9 8 7 6 5 4 3 2 1

MARVEL

ANT-MAN AND THE WASP

THE HEROES' JOURNEY

ADAPTED BY STEVE BEHLING
WRITTEN BY CHRIS McKENNA & ERIK SOMMERS
AND PAUL RUDD & ANDREW BARRER
& GABRIEL FERRARI
DIRECTED BY PEYTON REED
PRODUCED BY KEVIN FEIGE, P.G.A.

Ⓛ Ⓑ

Little, Brown and Company
New York   Boston

R0453292341

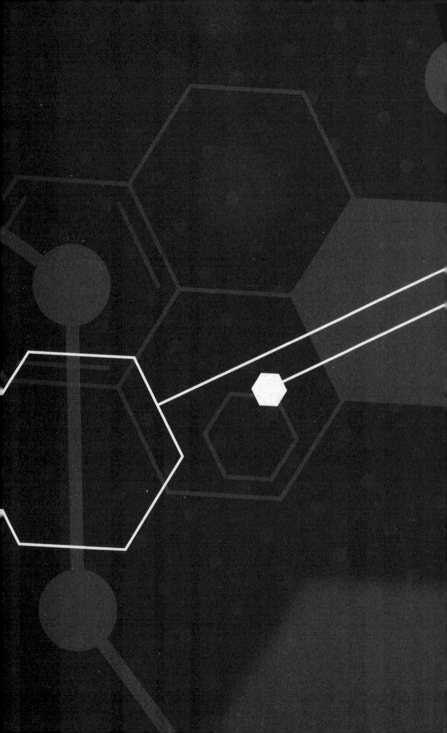

CHAPTER ONE

Do ants like spiders?"

Scott Lang absently scratched the back of his head as he considered the question. "I don't know," he answered. "I never really asked them. When I'm working with the ants, we don't really have a lot of time to just hang out and talk, get to know one another—"

"Well, do *you* like spiders?"

"Ah," Scott said, smiling at his ten-year-old daughter, Cassie. "I get where you're going with this. You're talking about that kid in the Captain America story, right?"

Cassie fidgeted in her chair, her bright, open face breaking out in a broad grin. Scott knew what that meant. It was story time again.

"I mean…He was okay. I guess. Really polite, actually. I bet his family would be proud. I didn't like what he did to me, but we were all kind of fighting, so I guess it was fair," Scott said.

"What did he do to you?" Cassie asked, still smiling at her father in anticipation as she took a big bite of a peanut butter and jelly sandwich. She loved to ask Scott questions, even when she already knew the answers.

"C'mon, Peanut, I told you this story before. You know what he did," Scott said.

His daughter simply grinned, chewing the soft whole-wheat bread and wiping her mouth with the paper napkin she clutched in her right hand. Cassie took another bite. This time, loud crunching sounds came from her mouth as she chewed.

Scott looked at his daughter and raised his right eyebrow. "Did you put corn chips on your sandwich again?"

"Mmmmaybe," Cassie said, her mouth full of food. Scott couldn't help laughing. He got up from the table in the tiny kitchen of his town house and walked over to the counter to make himself a sandwich, too.

"Don't forget the corn chips," Cassie said in between bites. "They're the best part. Can you tell me more stories?"

Scott set down two pieces of bread on the counter

and glanced over at the table. Cassie had opened the sandwich on her plate and was using two corn chips to scoop out the remaining peanut butter and jelly.

Scott twisted his face into a playful frown. "So gross," he said, his voice bursting with affection and pride. He wouldn't have it any other way.

———————◇———————

Scott relished the days when Cassie visited him. He was a man of many talents, but he thought his best talent—his all-time favorite ability, really—was being Cassie's dad. She was so smart, so funny, and so warm. The girl meant the world to him. He would do anything for her. Even if that meant making gross peanut butter and jelly (and corn chip) sandwiches.

Times like these were few and far between now. A few years back, Scott and his wife, Maggie—Cassie's mom—had gotten a divorce. Now Cassie lived with her mom and stepdad full time, and she visited Scott on the weekends. Their situation made it tough for Scott to foster anything resembling a normal, healthy father/daughter relationship.

Then, on top of that, there was his criminal record.

Oh yeah. *That.*

Currently, Scott was...How had his friend Luis put

it? "Enjoying the prolonged and enforced hospitality of his home." Luis always tried to put a good face on things.

Unfortunately, the federal authorities had another name for it: "house arrest." All because of the Captain America thing. Which wasn't even really his fault, because who says no to Captain America?

Exactly.

But as a result of that whole fiasco, Scott now had to stay inside his town house and wear an ankle monitor at all times. He couldn't take it off, not even to shower, or a swarm of federal agents would be on him like bees on honey.

That had actually happened before. It was about a week or so after he was first placed under house arrest. He woke up one morning, groggy, and decided that he was going to walk outside and get the newspaper so he could read it with breakfast. He opened the front door, and still half asleep, saw the newspaper on the sidewalk. Without thinking, he walked across the lawn and set one foot on the concrete sidewalk, and the ankle monitor went kablooey. A few minutes later, multiple black sedans pulled up in front of the apartment, tires screeching.

And a swarm of federal agents were on him like blah blah blah. You get the picture.

They read him the riot act for even so much as *thinking* about stepping outside the yard, reminding Scott that it was in direct violation of his sentence. The authorities let him off with a very stern warning that time, along with a reminder that if he ever did that again, he could forget all about house arrest and go back to San Quentin prison, where he probably should have been in the first place.

The really embarrassing part of that whole situation? It wasn't even his newspaper. Because Scott forgot that he didn't have home delivery.

Typical Lang luck.

"Are you thinking again, Daddy?" Cassie asked after she swallowed a mouthful of apple juice.

"Huh?" Scott said, a little dazed. "Oh. Yeah, I was, a little bit."

"About telling me a story?" Cassie said hopefully.

"Yeah, definitely," Scott sighed as he finished spreading peanut butter on one slice of bread and jammed the other slice of bread down on top of it. He wasn't a jelly guy—or a corn chips guy, for that matter. "You wanna hear the Captain America story?"

CHAPTER TWO

The Captain America story" was Cassie's name for what happened to Scott when he left San Francisco and headed to Germany to help Captain America.

The Captain America.

Scott couldn't believe it at the time. He was just an ordinary guy. He certainly didn't consider himself to be a Super Hero, like Captain America or any of the Avengers. He was just Scott Lang, engineer, former burglar, a guy who just happened to be in the wrong place at the wrong time, who had acquired a shrinking suit from a grizzled old scientist who used to work for S.H.I.E.L.D., and had become Ant-Man, picking up the mantle from said old scientist.

So typical.

It was right after Scott had first become the new Ant-Man (which Cassie called "The Ant-Man Story," appropriately enough). He had just defeated a guy named Darren Cross, saved Cassie, and turned an ant into the size of a large dog. And he was hanging out with Luis, who supposedly had a hot tip for Scott.

Scott knew he was in for it, because when Luis started talking, things tended to get confusing. Fast.

"So I'm at this art museum with my cousin Ignacio, right?" Luis began. "And there was this, like, abstract expressionism exhibit, and you know me, I'm more of a neo-cubist kind of guy, right?"

Where is this going? Scott thought.

"But there was this one that was sublime, bro!"

"Luis," Scott interjected, trying to get his friend back on track. He liked art as much as the next person, but this wasn't the time and place for a discussion about abstract expressionist painting.

"Okay. Sorry, sorry," Luis apologized. "You know I just get excited and stuff. But anyway, Ignacio tells me, 'Yo! I met this crazy-fine writer chick at the Spot last night. Like, *fine*-fine.' So this writer chick tells Ignacio, 'Yo! I'm, like, a boss in the world of guerrilla journalism, and I got mad connects with the peeps behind the curtains, you know what I'm sayin'?'"

Scott remained silent.

"Ignacio's like, 'For real?' And she's like, 'Yeah, you know what, I can't tell you who my contact is, because he works with the Avengers.'"

"Oh no," Scott sighed. He had a sinking feeling in

the pit of his stomach. On one of his first missions as Ant-Man, he had broken into an old Stark Enterprises facility in upstate New York to get something for Hank Pym. Only it wasn't an old Stark Enterprises facility anymore. It was an Avengers facility.

And Falcon had been there.

And Ant-Man had fought Falcon. And actually won. Falcon wasn't happy about that.

This was not looking good.

Luis explained that a pretty weird guy approached the journalist. "He said, 'Yo, I'm looking for this dude who's new on the scene, who's flashing his fresh tech, who's got, like, bomb moves, right? Who you got?' And she's like, 'Well, we got everything nowadays. We got a guy who jumps. We got a guy who swings, we got a guy who crawls up the walls. *You gotta be more specific.*' And he's like, 'I'm looking for a guy that *shrinks.*'"

Scott sighed again, but there was nothing he could do. Conversations with Luis were like being on an express train. You hopped on, and there were no stops until you reached your destination.

"And I got all nervous 'cause I'd keep mad secrets for you, bro!" Luis said to Scott. "So I asked Ignacio, 'Did that dude tell the stupid-fine writer chick to tell you to

tell me, because I'm tight with Ant-Man, that he's looking for him?'"

"And?" Scott said, waiting for it. "What'd he say?"

"He said, 'Yes!'"

It was a long way to go for a short drink of water, but
the point was made clear: The Avengers were looking
for Scott.

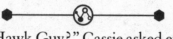

"What about Hawk Guy?" Cassie asked excitedly. "Isn't
he the one who took you to meet Captain America?"

"It's Hawkeye," Scott corrected, "And no one really
calls him that, honey. You can call him Mr. Barton.
He's a nice guy."

Once Scott knew that the Avengers were looking
for him, it was only a matter of time before he was
tracked down by one of their number—Clint Barton,
ace archer and former S.H.I.E.L.D. agent. There was
no call, no e-mail, no nothing. Just Barton, showing up
on his doorstep, telling him that he had to leave with
him. Now.

"He vouches for you, and that's good enough for
me," Barton had told him. "He" was Falcon, aka Sam
Wilson.

"But me? Really?" Scott had asked. "What about

Hulk or one of those guys? Wouldn't Captain America want a really strong guy?"

Barton had shrugged his shoulders. "Asked for you specifically, by name," he said. "You want to question Captain America's decisions?"

Scott had shaken his head vigorously. "No. Nope. I'm good with it," he replied quickly. "I'm gonna... Do I need to pack anything? Germany, what's the weather like this time of year?"

"Just yourself and your suit," Barton said. "There's a toothbrush on the quinjet with your name on it."

"Really?" Scott asked.

Barton smirked. "No."

The sound of the van door slamming into place woke Scott up with a start. He bolted upright on the back seat, where he'd fallen asleep.

"Man, what time zone is this?" Scott asked Barton.

"Come on," Barton said, patting Scott on the back as he got out of the van. "Come on." Then he gave Scott a little shove.

Standing right in front of him, inside an airport parking garage in Germany, was Steve Rogers.

Captain America.

Scott was in awe. He smiled, extended his right hand, and started to shake the hand of a living legend.

"Captain America!" Scott said, dumbfounded.

"Mr. Lang," Steve answered, his tone even.

"It's an honor," Scott said, his body bursting with nervous energy. "I'm shaking your hand too long. Wow. This is awesome!" Then he turned around and saw Wanda Maximoff, also known as Scarlet Witch. "I know you, too," he said to the woman with the red hair. "You're great!"

Scott really had no idea how he should act around other so-called Super Heroes. And he really didn't know how he should act around Captain America. That guy was a hero everyone looked up to! And now here Scott was, standing right in front of a man who fought the Red Skull, had been frozen for seventy years, and was one of the founding Avengers. "Look," Scott said, trying to sound cool, "I wanna say, I know you know a lot of super people, so thinks for thanking of me!"

No sooner had the words escaped his mouth than Scott realized he sounded like a tremendous doofus. Steve Rogers was classy enough to not say anything; he just nodded and smiled.

Scott then spotted a familiar face behind Captain

America. Eager to change the subject, he waved and said, "Hey, man!"

"What's up, Tic Tac?" Sam Wilson replied with a sharp nod of his head.

"Good to see you. Look, what happened last time—" Scott started to say. He felt the need to apologize for the brief encounter he'd had with Sam Wilson.

"It was a great audition, but it'll never happen again," Sam said confidently.

"They tell you what we're up against?" Steve asked.

"Something about some psycho assassins?" Scott answered, and it sounded like he hadn't really been paying attention.

"We're outside the law on this one," Steve said seriously. "So if you come with us, you're a wanted man."

Scott weighed Steve's words, then shrugged. "Yeah, well, what else is new?"

Scott had tried to sound confident, collected, cool. But really, he was nervous. Not about helping Captain America—he was honored to do that. And definitely not about being outside the law—that was par for the course for him.

He was nervous about Hope Van Dyne.

His friend and, more recently, his unofficial partner as the Wasp.

What was she going to say when she found out that he was taking the Ant-Man suit on an "unauthorized mission" outside the law without running it by the team?

What was *Hank*, inventor of the Ant-Man suit—not to mention the first to wear it—and Hope's father, going to say when he found out?

After the whole business with Darren Cross, the three had developed a sort of understanding among themselves: stay quiet; fly (literally) under the radar; keep everything on the down low.

Running off to Germany to join Captain America on his latest mission without even so much as mentioning it to Hope and Hank had definitely been a violation of that understanding. But there hadn't been time to loop them in.

And let's face it, Scott thought. *It's not like you're gonna pick up the phone and say, "Hey, Hope, I'm gonna take the Ant-Man suit out for a spin...be back in a few days."*

So Scott did what he did best—he made the decision and didn't look back.

CHAPTER THREE

Hank Pym was getting on Hope Van Dyne's nerves.

Again.

Granted, it took very little for that to happen. Being his daughter, Hope should have been used to it by now. But these days, it seemed as if it took almost nothing to set her off. Maybe it was being cooped up day after day with no one to talk to other than her father.

Or maybe it was having time to think. Too much time alone with her thoughts just gave Hope license to dwell on the same things over and over. To think about everything.

No. Not everything.

Her mother.

And maybe she was just plain angry.

"You haven't said a word all morning," Hank said, without looking up from the microscope. "Am I to take it that you're displeased?"

"'Displeased'?" Hope sputtered, erupting. "I don't think 'displeased' even begins to cover it."

"You're speaking," Hank replied as he looked up from the microscope. "That's progress."

"Progress is going to look an awful lot like me taking that microscope and—"

Hank put up both his hands, palms outward, in a gesture of surrender. "I've been a jerk."

Hope gazed up at the ceiling, searching for the words she wanted to say. "It's not about you being a jerk," she said slowly.

"I notice you didn't dispute the fact that I'm a jerk."

"It's about you just...not being there at all. Sitting here, holed up in this lab with you, it's just...it just reminds me of growing up," Hope said, the corners of her mouth turning downward. "It was lonely. And even when you were there, you weren't *there*."

The room remained silent for a while. Hope looked at her father, wanting him to say something, anything, that would change the past and make the present better. She knew that was impossible.

"I'm sorry," Hank said, his voice quiet. "I can't change what happened. All I can do is try to be here for you now."

"I know," she said, not sure whether she wanted to

give her dad a hug or punch him in the mouth. "But that doesn't make me any less angry."

Growing up the only child of Hank Pym and Janet Van Dyne, Hope was used to her parents being away, always leaving her in the care of a nanny or trusted friend. Sometimes it was just for a day or two. Other times, it was for weeks on end. Hope could have sworn they were gone for an entire year once, but that was probably just what it felt like to her.

Other kids her age had parents who worked, sure. But Hope's parents were different. Her father was a scientist who worked for S.H.I.E.L.D., the Strategic Homeland Intervention, Enforcement, and Logistics Division. He had logged plenty of time in a laboratory, where he developed what came to be known as Pym Particles—subatomic particles with a most unique property. When exposed to other matter, the Pym Particles could cause the object or being to grow smaller or larger. It was an incredible breakthrough, one that had the potential to change the course of human history.

And it would have, if Hank Pym had allowed someone other than himself to use the Pym Particles.

Hank knew just how dangerous and destabilizing

the power of shrinking and growing at will could be. What if someone were able to miniaturize a spy or an army? A nuclear weapon? What about making that same weapon the size of a house? The very notion of security was meaningless in a world where virtually anything could be shrunk down smaller than a pinhead or enlarged like Jack's giant beanstalk.

So Hank kept the secret of the Pym Particles—what made them tick—to himself. But that didn't mean he didn't use that secret for the benefit of others. Not only was he a S.H.I.E.L.D. scientist, but in time, Hank became an operative of the organization as well. He created a suit that enabled him to survive the stress and pressure of the shrinking process. His superiors dubbed him "Ant-Man" due to his size-changing capabilities. And it was decided that Ant-Man could help solve some pretty big problems.

And somewhere along the way, as Hank was missing from home for longer and longer stretches of time, Hope's mother convinced Hank that she should join him. Ant-Man needed a partner, someone to watch his back, some-one with whom he could trust his secret...and his life.

The argument won Hank over, and soon Janet had her own special suit. She was code-named Wasp and proved to be every bit as tenacious as her namesake.

If Hope had known at that young age that her parents were basically globe-trotting secret agents, she might have thought it was pretty cool. It might have made her miss them just a little less while they were gone.

But she didn't know. All she knew was, sometimes, Mommy and Daddy went away, and it was a long time before they came home.

And then there was the day that Daddy came home, and Mommy didn't.

The lab was stuffy, and Hope was getting sick of it. It seemed as if they were packing up and moving to a different location every day. And thanks to Hank's genius, that's quite literally what they had been doing. The laboratory was designed to be portable. In a way, it had a lot in common with the tiny home craze, where people built small houses that could be towed practically anywhere on trailers. Except in this case, Hank was able to shrink the laboratory with Pym Particles and attach a handle to the lab so it could accompany them wherever they went.

Our work, Hope thought with dismay. *We've been toiling night and day, and I can't tell if we're getting closer or further away.*

"We're going to have to move again soon," Hope said

out loud. She wasn't talking to Hank, and she wasn't talking to herself. She wasn't quite sure to whom she was talking, actually.

"Another day, another secluded location removed from prying eyes," Hank replied. He stood up from the microscope and walked over to an apparatus that looked like a large, metallic window frame.

"We're going to need that new part soon," he murmured, looking at their handiwork. "Of course it would have been easier to get that part if we didn't have to sneak around like—"

"Criminals?" Hope said bitterly. She knew something about criminals. Or rather, criminal, singular.

Scott Lang.

It was *his* fault that Hope was stuck in this little lab with her father, forced to move around to stay one step ahead of the law.

His fault that the project she and Hank were working on was taking so long to complete.

More waiting.

She had spent her whole life waiting.

Hope was tired of waiting.

CHAPTER FOUR

Tell me about Ant-Man again!" Cassie said. She had finished her sandwich and was now opening a plastic cup containing chocolate and vanilla ice cream. Scott had one, too. They each held a little wooden spoon in their hands as they started to dig into the dessert with relish. Maggie would flip her lid if she knew what passed as a "well-balanced meal" in Scott's house, but, hey, he had limited time with Cassie. If corn chips and ice cream sweetened the deal, who was he to deny his one and only daughter?

"I was in the middle of telling you the Captain America story," Scott protested. "Don't you want me to finish that one first?"

Cassie turned her head to the left, then right.

"So that's a no?" Scott asked.

"Tell me about Ant-Man, then you can tell me about Captain America again," Cassie said through a mouthful of ice cream. "I like your stories."

Scott slapped his knees with his hands, then stood up from the table. "The Ant-Man story it is," he said.

There was a reason that Scott and Maggie had gotten divorced. He always left this part out of the Ant-Man story when he told it to Cassie. But it was always there in the back of Scott's mind when he told it to her.

Scott was a good man and a good husband. And when he found out that he and Maggie were expecting a child, he knew that he would be a good father, too. Things were looking up.

Then, there was the Vistacorp job.

That was another part of the Ant-Man story that Scott had never told Cassie about—his side hustle as a burglar. But a righteous burglar, like a modern-day Robin Hood. The thing was, Scott couldn't stand to see people being ripped off or hurt by big corporations. Just the idea of people who couldn't fight for themselves, losing their life savings as corrupt companies essentially stole from them, made Scott angry. And when he got angry, he decided to do something about it.

In the case of Vistacorp, Scott had discovered that the company was deliberately overcharging its customers. So Scott hacked Vistacorp's systems and stole the money that they had stolen, and gave it back to the customers.

This made Scott feel good—he knew he was doing the right thing.

Unfortunately, the law saw things a bit differently. And while everyone agreed that his intentions were noble, the end result was that he had been stealing. Like a common thief.

So, unlike Robin Hood, Scott had been sent to San Quentin prison for three years.

Cassie was only little when Scott went away. While he was gone, Maggie divorced him. She had learned to live with Scott's Robin Hood act, but the Vistacorp job was one jump too far. Maggie needed stability in her life—not just for her, but for their daughter. She couldn't understand why Scott didn't want that, too.

Scott couldn't understand it, either. How had he messed up so bad? He loved Cassie more than anything. Why hadn't he thought through the consequences of his actions? Couldn't he have seen that pulling stunts like the Vistacorp job would lead down a lonely path?

Apparently not.

⬡————⊗————⬡

"So, when you got back from your business trip, you met up with Luis, and you went on an adventure! Tell me that part again!" Cassie said, wiggling in her seat.

The "business trip" was how Scott referred to San Quentin. He wasn't particularly proud of that deception, but he wasn't ready to explain everything that had happened.

"Right, so there I was, and I was looking for a job. And Luis had—"

"Hey hey hey! I'm right here!" Luis said, suddenly poking his head into Scott's room.

"Geez, don't you knock?" Scott asked, startled. "What were you doing, standing outside my room?"

Luis gave a sheepish grin. "Yeah. I like your stories, too. They're good. I mean, you get right to the point. I wish I could do that. But I just have to go with how I'm feeling, you know?" Luis said.

Scott gave a sort of half grin.

"So, you telling the part where we broke—"

Scott's eyes shot daggers at Luis as he subtly shook his head.

"Broke what?" Cassie asked.

Luis looked at Cassie for a moment, and Scott knew that his friend was choosing his next words very carefully. "We broke it down," Luis said. "'Cause I have mad skills. Like, I can do it right now, you with me?"

Cassie started to laugh, and Scott sighed heavily with relief. Luis was going to be the death of him.

———•———⊗———•———

It was a simple job. Not as simple as the job he'd had working at an ice-cream shop, but that opportunity fell through when management found out about his criminal record. (As Luis told him, *Ice cream always finds out*.) Even though Scott was an electrical engineer, he found out just how difficult it was to find steady work with that prison sentence in his past. The shop had been a brief reprieve in an otherwise unemployed first few months back out on the job scene.

According to Luis, there was this mansion that had a huge safe in the basement, all of which signified big bucks. All Scott had to do was join Luis and his partners Kurt and Dave, break into the big house, crack the big safe, and take the big bucks.

At this point, Scott had sworn that he would never pull a job again. If he were caught, it would be right back to prison, and there would be no way Maggie would ever allow him to see Cassie again. But the flip side of it was this: If Scott wanted to see Cassie now, he had to pay child support to Maggie. And if he were going to pay child support, he needed a steady job. But he couldn't get a steady job because of his criminal record.

It was a vicious cycle.

And Scott knew there was only one way to break it: by pulling one more job.

So imagine Scott's surprise when he cracked the safe and found exactly zero dollars and zero cents inside. All he found was a funky-looking motorcycle helmet and leathers. He grabbed them so the night wouldn't be a total loss, except that it was.

When the group got back to the apartment they all shared, Scott was disappointed. Not in the job, but in himself. He had sworn never to commit another crime, and, yet, he had done exactly that. No matter how much he told himself it was for a noble cause—ensuring he could see his daughter so she could have her father—Scott couldn't shake the feeling that he had somehow failed Cassie in the worst way possible.

Alone in the apartment, Scott contemplated his face in the mirror. He looked at the motorcycle helmet and leathers and decided to try them on. He wasn't sure why, exactly. But he put them on and was surprised at how snugly the jumpsuit fit. He put on the helmet. It wasn't like any motorcycle helmet he had ever seen before.

Taking a few steps back from the mirror, Scott stood in the bathtub, trying to get a better look at himself. The outfit looked weird. Kinda buggy, if he were being honest. There was definitely something…insect-like about it. Was this even a real helmet?

He noticed there were controls on each of his gloved hands—a button on the left hand and a button on the right. Scott pressed the button on the left hand, and nothing happened. Then he pressed the one on the right hand and, in the wink of an eye, Scott's world grew bigger.

Because Scott was growing smaller.

In the space between seconds, from the moment Scott pressed that button, he shrank to the size of an ant. A literal ant. And now he was at the bottom of the bathtub, standing right next to the drain, which loomed enormous before him like a gigantic, gaping pit.

So he did what anyone in his position would have done.

He. Freaked. Out.

And at that moment, Scott heard the voice of Hank Pym for the first time.

"The world sure seems different from down here, doesn't it, Scott?"

The voice exploded in Scott's ears, and it sounded more than a little condescending.

"Who said that?" Scott shouted, looking around. But there was no one there—until Luis walked into the bathroom and parted the shower curtain. He looked like a giant.

Scott did everything he could think of to draw Luis's attention to his predicament, jumping up and down, waving, yelling at the top of his lungs. But it was no use—he was just too tiny. Luis couldn't see him or hear him.

And Luis was about to turn on the shower.

"It's a trial by fire, Scott," the voice said, filling Scott's ears. "Or in this case... water."

A roaring fountain gushed from the faucet toward Scott. It looked like Armageddon. He started to run in the opposite direction as a wall of water formed behind him and threatened to sweep him up. The water surged, and Scott found himself lifted off his feet, helpless, until he was thrown clear of the bathtub.

He landed on the tile floor like an anvil, smashing an ant-size divot into the floor.

"I guess you're tougher than you thought," said the voice.

CHAPTER FIVE

Scott's story was interrupted mid-sentence by a phone call from Jimmy Woo.

"Agent Woo?" Scott said into his phone. "Did I do something? I haven't left the apartment, I swear. The ankle monitor is on, and I am—"

"Relax, Mr. Lang, you're fine," said Agent Woo. "It's just time for our daily check-in. I'm in the field on another assignment, so I'm calling it in today."

"Oh, okay," Scott answered with palpable relief. Woo made him nervous. He hoped he didn't sound nervous, but he was pretty sure that he did. "Well, I'm here at home, not leaving, like usual."

"Good," Woo replied, clearly distracted. "Because I'd hate for anything to ruin our arrangement. I'm sure Cassie would hate it, too. You're so close, Scott. It's only a matter of time before your sentence is served."

Scott hated it whenever anyone brought Cassie into the conversation like that. As far as he was concerned, talking about Cassie was off-limits, unless it was to mention how cool she was, or how cute she was, or how smart she was.

"I'm not gonna do anything to mess up my situation," Scott said, exasperation creeping into his voice. "Not after what I've been through."

The reason for the house arrest all came down to a little violation. By accompanying Clint Barton to Germany and helping Captain America, Scott had found himself in violation of article 16, paragraph 3 of the Sokovia Accords. The Sokovia Accords were a global agreement, signed by 117 countries, governing the operations of so-called super-powered individuals, like the Avengers.

As part of a plea deal with the US Department of Homeland Security and the German government, Scott had been allowed to return to the United States and serve a two-year sentence under house arrest. As part of his agreement, Scott also had to swear that he would have no contact with any former associates who were currently in violation of the Sokovia Accords.

Like Hank Pym and Hope Van Dyne.

When he went off to Germany to fight alongside Captain America, Scott didn't realize the consequences of his actions. Even when Cap himself told Scott that they were outside the law on the operation, and it could land Scott back in prison.

Dumb, Lang, he thought. *Dumb.*

"Are you even listening to me?"

"Huh? What?" Scott asked.

"I—wait, there's someone here who…no, I haven't… what, Scott?" Jimmy Woo asked.

Scott pulled the phone away from his face and looked at the thin, black rectangle in his hand. *Why are we even having this conversation?* he thought. *Neither one of us is paying attention.*

"Listen, Agent Woo, I have to go now," Scott said, winking at Cassie. "These corn chips aren't going to eat themselves."

"Right, right," Woo answered, distracted. "Well, keep your nose clean. Talk with you tomorrow."

Scott disconnected the call, then let out a long, heavy sigh. Cassie leaned over and gave her father a big hug that actually hurt his rib cage a little.

"You're getting strong, Peanut," Scott said.

"Strong like the Hulk!" Cassie giggled as she flexed her muscles and made an angry-looking face. Suddenly, her face became very serious. "Did you ever fight the Hulk? Did you?"

"No, honey, I never fought the Hulk," Scott said. He could see that Cassie looked a little disappointed. "But I met a guy who did."

"Really?" Cassie said, brightening. "Who?"

"Iron Man," Scott replied.

"I still don't understand why *you* had to fight Iron Man," Cassie said, her voice suddenly serious. "I didn't like that."

"I didn't like it, either," Scott said.

CHAPTER SIX

Sneaking around like a criminal was not something that appealed to Hope in the slightest. She doubted she would ever get used to it and prayed that she wouldn't have to.

Throwing a roundhouse kick at the practice dummy with her left leg, Hope felt her foot connect. The solid hit brought a certain calm to her. So she wound up and threw another with her right leg. If the practice dummy could talk, it would be begging for mercy.

It wouldn't get any. Even if it could talk.

The more she thought about her situation, the faster the blows came. First her right arm, then her left, hands lashing out at the dummy. With ruthless efficiency, she attacked the dummy's upper and lower arms, landing an occasional hit in its chest for good measure.

It wasn't enough for her.

So she launched into another series of punches, more precise than the last. She was picking different parts of the practice dummy, pinpointing areas where she wanted to inflict maximum damage.

Head.

Shoulders.

Chest.

It was an incredible release, losing herself in training. An escape. More than that, by focusing her body and mind on constantly honing her fighting abilities, Hope was keeping her eyes on the prize. Looking down the road toward the day when she would don her own special suit—and become the Wasp.

As she worked out, another thought crossed her mind. That she might already have had her chance to prove herself as the Wasp if it hadn't been for Scott.

Good ol' Scott Lang. In light of recent events, Hope found herself questioning Hank's wisdom in approaching Scott to join them in the first place.

Things had started off promisingly enough. She and Scott worked well together. Together with her father, the three had destroyed Darren Cross's mad and dangerous dream of selling shrinking technology to the highest bidder, creating a world in which miniaturized mercenaries could attack and destabilize a country before they could even react. The battle with Cross had been fought in public in front of lots of witnesses. Those witnesses saw Pym Technologies literally implode before their eyes, for all intents and purposes disappearing into apparent nothingness.

The Quantum Realm.

We could have been there by now, Hope thought bitterly. *We could have found her. Except for Scott...*

Head.

Shoulders.

Chest.

Roundhouse kick.

Poor dummy. Scott.

After what had happened with Darren and Pym Technologies, Hank had ordered Scott to lie low. "Keep a tight lid on it," was how he put it. Hank didn't want any federal agency sniffing around, trying to get their hands on his tech. As far as Hank was concerned, there would be no more risks, and that meant no more appearances—public or otherwise—from Ant-Man.

Hope knew that her father was worried about his tech falling into the wrong hands, to be sure; but the real reason behind his instructions to Scott was that Hank wouldn't allow anything to happen that could jeopardize what might be the only chance they had to rescue Hope's mother.

Hope grabbed a towel and wiped her brow.

The practice dummy lay in pieces at her feet.

— ● —————— ◆ —————— ● —

Even the memory made Hope's throat clench. Thinking back to when her father at last opened up to her, telling her what happened to her mother, caused her to fight back tears.

She had been furious with her father when he'd first recruited Scott to wear the Ant-Man suit, not that being angry with Hank was anything new. Hope had wanted to be Ant-Man, to sneak inside Pym Technologies and steal the Yellowjacket suit from Cross. Hadn't she proved herself capable, over and over again? Why wouldn't her father trust her to do this, and why would he put his faith in a burglar like Scott Lang instead, someone he hardly even knew?

She was at the end of her rope. A part of her had believed that working with Hank to stop Cross would bring them together, and help close the seemingly unbridgeable gap between them.

But another part of Hope had thought she was dead wrong.

That's when Scott said something that changed her way of thinking.

"I'm expendable," Scott had explained to her as she hid in her car, alone with her rage and disappointment. "That's why I'm here. You must have realized that by now. I mean, that's why I'm in the suit and you're not. He'd rather lose this fight than lose you."

Hope hadn't thought of it that way. Why would she? For her entire life, all she knew about her father was that he'd tried to shut her out of his life.

When she went back inside Hank's house to confront him, Hope could never have expected what was coming.

With his back to her, Hank slowly began to speak.

"Your mother," Hank began, "convinced me to let her join me on my...missions. They called her the Wasp. She was born to it."

Hope listened, hanging on every word.

"And there's not a day that goes by that I don't regret having said yes."

For a moment, it seemed as if Hank were unable to continue, the words simmering just beneath the surface. Then, quietly: "It was 1987. Separatists had hijacked a Soviet missile silo in Kursk and launched an ICBM at the United States."

Hope remained silent, willing her father to continue.

"The only way to the internal mechanics was through solid titanium. I knew I had to shrink between the molecules to disarm the missile. But my regulator had sustained too much damage," Hank said, his voice quivering. "Your mother...she didn't hesitate. She turned off her regulator and went subatomic...to deactivate the bomb. And she was gone."

Hope had never heard the story before, never known what had really happened to her mother. And she had never seen her father like this. Raw and vulnerable.

"Your mom died a hero," he said, looking at Hope, searching her eyes for...understanding? Forgiveness? "And I spent the next ten years trying to learn all I could about the Quantum Realm."

Through her tears, Hope nodded, at last understanding. "You were trying to bring her back," she said.

Hank gave a small nod. "But all I learned was we know nothing."

That may have been the case back then, the Quantum Realm remaining an impenetrable mystery to Hank despite years of research and experimentation. But after the Yellowjacket affair, they had learned something. In order to defeat Cross, Scott had needed to go subatomic and destroy the Yellowjacket suit from the inside out. Just as Janet had all those years ago, shrinking and shrinking, slipping between molecules, Scott became smaller and smaller until he could do what was required to rid the world of Yellowjacket—and the threat he presented—forever.

Darren had imploded. There was nothing left of him—not a sign, not a trace. Scott, on the other hand, had continued to shrink, until he found himself drifting in the netherworld of the Quantum Realm.

Only through a supreme act of will and a lot of luck, after hearing Cassie calling for him, had Scott found a way to enlarge himself, escaping the Quantum Realm.

To Hope, and to Hank, the feat of returning from the Quantum Realm nearly outweighed the value of defeating Yellowjacket himself. Scott had been to the Quantum Realm and back. He had survived.

If Scott could travel there and back...if he could survive...

...so could Janet.

After the Yellowjacket affair, Hank and Hope devoted themselves to finding a way to reach the Quantum Realm and return alive—and with Janet in tow. They worked quietly, under the radar, using Hank's resources to fund the project. Based on what they had learned from Scott, they were making progress. They were maybe less than a year away from perfecting the Quantum Tunnel, as Hank had christened it. In less than a year, they would have a way to explore the Quantum Realm safely, to try to find Hope's mother and bring her home.

Until Scott ruined everything.

As usual.

CHAPTER SEVEN

How did *Scott manage to ruin everything?* Hope thought. It was infuriating—all it had taken was one man to make one rash decision to jeopardize everything she and Hank had been working for.

Hank couldn't have been more explicit or direct—"keep a tight lid on it." Meaning, "Don't take the Ant-Man suit out for a joyride; don't attract unwanted attention." Anyone with half a brain would have understood what that meant—and listened.

Yet, somehow, Scott had managed to do both. In a very public, very problematic way.

What really irked Hope, what really got under her skin, was how Scott didn't even say a word to her about the mission he had so casually accepted before he left. As if it hadn't even occurred to him that there might be a problem, and maybe he should ask her opinion about what he should do. After everything they had been through together, Hope thought...Well, what *did* she think? That they trusted each other? That they cared about each other?

If you care about someone, and if you trust them, then how can they just sneak away like that? Hope wondered.

So while she and Hank had been toiling in his basement laboratory, trying to perfect the tech needed to make the Quantum Tunnel a reality, Scott had slunk off to Germany without anyone knowing.

And for what?

To be a hotshot part of some big Super Hero battle with Captain America and Iron Man, and a whole mess of others.

Even now, just thinking about Scott running off like that made Hope want to kick him in the jaw.

Hard.

Like almost everyone else on the planet, she and Hank had found out about it on the news. The first reports were coming out of the Leipzig–Halle Airport, southwest of Berlin. There was some kind of battle going on that could only be described as a massive-scale fight between Avengers. On one side, there was Iron Man, War Machine, Black Widow, Vision, and some skinny guy wearing a suit with a spider on it. On the other, there was Captain America, Falcon, Scarlet Witch, Hawkeye, the Winter Soldier, and...Scott Lang, aka Ant-Man.

Ant-Man, Hope thought, laughing bitterly. Maybe if Scott had been fighting in his tiny form, he wouldn't have been visible, and no one would have even known that he'd been taking part in the battle. That might have been forgivable. Then she would only have been angry at Scott for running off like some fan-boy just because Captain America came calling.

But Scott hadn't exactly appeared "ant size" on TV.

More like "giant economy size." In the time since the Yellowjacket affair, Hank had been conducting some research alongside Scott. And one of the things they had discovered was that if a person could use the Pym Particles to shrink and return to their normal size, then they could also use them to grow taller.

Like, really tall.

Size-of-a-building tall.

That was exactly what Scott had done, right in front of the cameras at the airport. There he was, throwing vehicles around as if they were toys, fighting Iron Man for all the world to see.

It seemed appropriate, Hope thought, that Scott should grow to giant size. In that way, he became the living embodiment for the giant-size problems that he had just caused for her and Hank.

With Pym's size-changing technology on global display, it was only a matter of time before the authorities—whether it was the FBI or the CIA, the remnants of S.H.I.E.L.D., or Hydra, or who knows what else—would come calling, looking to seize the technology, and Hope and Hank along with it.

When she saw him on TV, Hope had two separate and distinct reactions. First, she was speechless, staring at the screen, slack-jawed. She wanted to find her practice dummy and give it a thrashing, imagining Scott's face on the thing.

Then Hope decided to do what she did best.

Face things head-on.

"Gather whatever you can," Hope said as she walked into Hank's lab with purpose. Then she looked at a workbench and, with the sweep of her right arm, cleared it. "Put it all here."

Hope was walking through the lab, taking note of what they were going to need for their Quantum Tunnel project. The TV was blaring in the background, repeating the top news of the day, featuring big, dumb Scott Lang. She was placing small vials full of Pym Particles into a silver suitcase.

"What have you found out?" Hope asked.

Hank barely looked up from his workstation as he pored over an array of tools. His cell phone was sitting next to him.

"I just got off the phone with a contact of mine from my S.H.I.E.L.D. days. Says the federal authorities are already on their way here. Your plan is our only way out. We take everything we think we need to complete the Quantum Tunnel. And then we take everything we think we *won't* need, because we'll probably need that, too."

"And we shrink everything," Hope said, following her father's logic. "But where will we go? It's not like we can just check into a motel and build a Quantum Tunnel."

"No," Hank said, agreeing with Hope. "But I've prepared a little something just in case a situation like this ever came up."

"Thanks, Scott," Hope said. She didn't mean it.

"We'll deal with the brainless Boy Scout when he comes back," Hank said. "*If* he comes back. Lord knows what Ross will do with Scott and his new Super Hero pals. Probably throw them in the Raft." "Ross" was Thaddeus Ross, a retired general who was now the secretary of state. He was largely responsible for shepherding the Sokovia Accords through the US government. And he also oversaw "the Raft," a floating prison for super-powered individuals, located somewhere in the middle of the Atlantic Ocean.

"I think that's everything," Hope said, placing the silver suitcase down on the table. "Now what's the 'little something' you've prepared for this situation?"

Hank smiled. In his right hand, he grasped a small cube by its gleaming handle. "Your new home," he said.

CHAPTER EIGHT

"Yeah," Scott said as he dropped a red checker into place. "It hurts when Iron Man hits you."

"Even when you're teeny tiny, like an ant?" Cassie asked. She held a black checker in her left hand and stared at Scott with her big eyes.

"I don't know," Scott answered, "because he didn't hit me when I was ant size. I was big. Maybe if I had been ant size he wouldn't have been able to hit me at all."

While Scott was talking, Cassie made her move.

"Did you just drop two checkers at once?" Scott said, raising an eyebrow at his daughter. Cassie started to giggle.

"So? It's Connect 4, Daddy," Cassie said, taking two more checkers and placing them in the plastic grid.

"Yeah, but not all at once!" Scott protested and started laughing, too. It had been too long since he'd enjoyed time like this with Cassie. For a brief moment, he had been able to forget that he was under house arrest. It seemed like he was an average father, spending time with his daughter, playing games, talking, and just having fun.

But he knew their time together was fleeting. Soon, it would be time for Cassie to go back home to her mother. And Scott would once again be alone with the monitor he wore around his ankle 24/7 and his thoughts.

He didn't want to ruin the rest of Cassie's visit. But it was hard to keep the thoughts at bay for long.

"Why do you talk to ants?" Cassie asked innocently.

"Why? To tell them what to do," Scott said. "They're a big help."

Cassie started to put the game pieces back in the box. "No, I mean, why *ants*? Why not some other kind of bug?"

Scott looked at his daughter with pride. His daughter never failed to surprise him with her thoughtful, insightful questions and observations about the world around her. Cassie had an incredible natural curiosity imbedded in her. *She's definitely smarter than I was at her age,* he thought.

"I think Dr. Pym chose ants for a lot of good reasons. What do you think they are?" Scott asked.

The young girl immediately started to enumerate the potential reasons with the fingers on her right hand, letting Scott know she'd been contemplating this question for some time. "Ants are really strong," she said in a rush. "And they can talk to one another. And ants know how to work together really well."

"I'm gonna have to introduce you to Dr. Pym one day," Scott said, squeezing Cassie's shoulder. "That's right; those are all good reasons why he chose ants, I think."

"So how do you talk to them?" Cassie asked.

"How do I—? Well, it's kind of complicated...."

"You have to clear your mind, Scott."

Scott was sitting in the passenger seat of a car next to Hope. They were in Hank Pym's driveway. So far, he had been unable to communicate with the ants that Hank used in his missions as Ant-Man. And if Scott couldn't talk to the ants and get them to help...well, then he wasn't much of an Ant-Man, was he?

"You have to make your thoughts precise—that's how it works," Hope said, handing an earpiece to Scott. "Think about Cassie and how bad you want to see her, and use that to focus."

He wasn't sure if he could do it, but Scott figured he had nothing to lose. He took the earpiece and attached it to his right ear, the way Hope had shown him. Then he closed his eyes, took a deep breath, and released it.

Scott watched as Hope took a penny between her fingers and gently placed it on the dashboard in front of them.

"Open your eyes," Hope said quietly, "and just think about what you want the ants to do."

Scott did exactly that. Opening his eyes slowly, he thought about the ants coming through one of the seams in the dashboard and approaching the penny. A second or two ticked by, but to Scott, it might as well have been an hour.

Then he saw the first little black head peek out from the dashboard. It was a carpenter ant, and it started to move across the dashboard toward the penny. A moment later, it was joined by another carpenter ant. Then another. And finally, another.

The four ants walked right over to the penny while Scott looked at them, thinking about what he wanted the ants to do.

You're doing a great job, guys, Scott thought. *Now if you could just pick up the penny...*

As if Scott had just addressed them out loud, the ants used their heads, antennae, and front legs to manipulate the coin, picking it up off the dash. They now held the penny aloft.

Scott gasped audibly. He was actually communicating with the ants! It was unbelievable!

"That's good!" Hope said encouragingly.

Wondering just how far he could go, and what the ants were capable of, Scott stared at the ants for a moment. *Let's see what you guys can do,* he said. *Maybe you could give that penny a spin....*

That's precisely what the ants did. They spun the penny until it was standing vertically, whipping around in quick, circular motions.

Scott understood that he had just taken a step into a larger—yet paradoxically smaller—world.

"So the ants can do anything you ask them to?" Cassie said.

"Well, yeah, I guess. Within reason," Scott added. "I mean, they're not gonna do your homework, if that's what you're asking me."

Cassie laughed. "No way! I do my own homework!" She got up from the floor where both she and Scott had been sitting and put the game box back on a nearby shelf.

"What else do you want to play?" Scott asked. But

before Cassie could answer, Luis had poked his head into the room again.

"Scotty!" Luis said. "Cassie!"

"Hey, Luis," Scott said. Cassie just smiled in response.

"You remember how you told me to tell you if that thing ever became a problem?" Luis said.

"I literally have no idea what you're talking about," Scott said. "Could this wait until after I'm done playing with Cassie? She's gonna have to go home in, like, an hour...."

"Yeah, sure, an hour's fine. It's not like the business will totally tank in that time, and we'll have no jobs and no prospects—that's cool," Luis said, still smiling.

Scott glanced at Cassie, who was now sitting rapt with attention, laser-focused on Luis. She could tell by now when one of Luis's long-winded, often ludicrous stories was coming, and she loved them.

Scott sighed. "Okay, tell me."

CHAPTER NINE

Yo, so check it," Luis said. "So I'm at the gas station because they have those microwave cheeseburgers that I like, plus I have to get gas. So I'm like, 'Why not kill two birds with one stone, right?'"

Scott nodded. It was always safer just to nod when Luis was building steam. Luis loved nothing more than to hold the floor and relate his conversations in great detail.

Every.

Single.

Detail.

"And I'm eating a cheeseburger when I get a call and it's my friend Floyd. Now, I don't talk about Floyd much because of that thing that happened with the fish, but I think we moved past that, and he calls to tell me about this job."

Cassie looked at Luis, then at Scott, then back to Luis. She was grinning widely, enthralled.

"So I say, 'What kind of job?' and Floyd says, 'You know how you gonna start that security company?' and then I think, *Did I tell Floyd about our security company, because I don't remember telling him anything about it. But I could have, maybe, when—"*

"Try to get to the point, Luis," Scott said softly. "Breathe in, breathe out." Trying to keep Luis focused was often an exercise in frustration, but Scott had to try.

"Right, Scotty, right. So I say, 'Yeah, I know that security company,' and he says, 'Well, my brother, Lester, he's working for a company now that needs some security.' So I call Lester, and he says, 'Yeah, that's right. I know a guy who's working for a guy who needs some security right now, because he's doing lots of business with some shady types, and there's lots of technology involved.' "

"Mmm-hmmm," Scott said impassively.

"And you know when he said 'technology,' I thought of you automatically, because of all that technology stuff you like," Luis continued. "So I said, 'Lester, can you hook me up with this guy who's working for a guy and can you tell me his name?' and he says, 'No, I can't tell you his last name, or he'll kill me.' "

Scott's eyes went wide. He looked quickly at Cassie, and then glared at Luis as if to say, *Man, not in front of my kid.*

Luis picked up on Scott's nonverbal cue immediately.

"I mean, not literally kill; it was just, like, a figure of speech. Anyway, he says that this guy whose last name he can't say has been doing business with some people who used to work for some big technology company that went belly-up."

Pym Technologies? Scott wondered. *Or is that too much of a coincidence?*

"So I get Lester to tell me that the guy who everyone's working for is named Sonny, but no last name, and then I figured I needed to tell you, because maybe something's up and maybe there's an opportunity or maybe it's all just, like, bad trouble, and we should avoid it, or maybe it's already too late, and we can't avoid anything." When the last words poured out of Luis's mouth, he didn't even appear to be out of breath. He stood there, grinning, blinking once or twice at Scott.

What if the people Luis mentioned had worked for Pym Technologies? And what if those people...What if they were Hope and Hank?

That threw Scott for a loop.

He hadn't spoken with Hope or Hank since before everything had gone down in Germany. When he finally got home, he thought about calling them, especially Hope. But it was kind of a Catch-22 situation: He had no doubt she was angry with him, and he wanted to call her to find out *how* angry she was. But because he knew she was angry, he was afraid to call.

So, instead, he did nothing. Scott knew that he had disappointed Hope. And Scott found that very hard to live with.

"So, what do you know about this guy Sonny?" Scott asked.

Luis nodded vigorously, having anticipated the question. "He's a bad dude. Supplies things that people need for a price, and that price is really high. Like, we're not talking just money, but, like, blackmail and secrets and stuff like that, you know what I'm sayin'?"

"*I* know what you're saying!" Cassie said, jumping into the conversation.

Luis put up his right hand, inviting Cassie to give him a high five. The two slapped hands. "She's so smart, Scotty," Luis said, beaming at Cassie. "They grow up so fast."

"Yeah, they do," Scott said. "Can I talk to your friend's brother's guy who knows a guy?"

"You followed all that?" Luis said.

"Yeah," Scott replied. "I was actually paying attention. It wasn't that hard to follow."

"Right right. I'm just not used to anyone actually doing that, and being able to repeat in part or in whole the things that I've said. Excellent," Luis said enthusiastically.

"So can you get me in touch with that guy?" Scott asked.

Luis blinked. "What guy?"

Scott started to roll his eyes, when Luis cracked up. "I'm just messing with you. Yeah, I can find out where he works, then we can go—" Halting in mid-sentence, Luis looked down at Scott's leg, at the ankle monitor. "Or I can get a number, and you can call."

There was a beat of silence. "Calling works best," Scott said.

CHAPTER TEN

t's always Sonny," Hope said, her tone tinged with disgust. She had spoken the name *Sonny* as if it were a curse. That's how it felt to her.

"He's a necessary evil," Hank replied, matter-of-fact, eyes focused on the road ahead of him. "Do you think I would have anything to do with him if there was another way? We're all out of options, thanks to that boyfriend of yours."

Hope bit her bottom lip and looked out the window. She could feel her right hand balling up into a fist. Not this again. "He's not my 'boyfriend,'" Hope said, and even she could practically hear the sound of her eyes rolling. "And even if he were, which he's not, that's all in the past. It's not like we can go back in time and prevent Scott from heading overseas to pal around with Captain America."

Hank laughed. "I suppose not. Are you all set for the meeting?" he asked, and Hope detected a trace of nervousness in his voice.

Truth be told, Hope was a little nervous as well. Since going incognito, she and Hank had found that working on the Quantum Tunnel was easier said than done. The things they took for granted before—such as easy access to materials, working space, and the ability to move around freely—were now beyond reach. When she went out in public, *if* she went out in public, Hope was always looking over her shoulder, always in some sort of disguise. Was the person standing in line next to her at the supermarket really there to buy orange juice and a box of donuts, or was he some kind of government stooge waiting to pounce?

Hope watched as the rows of houses outside the van window started to thin, leading to a small business district. Most of the shop windows had FOR LEASE or STORE CLOSED signs posted. It wasn't exactly a thriving spot.

Thanks to Scott, she and Hank had to find another way to obtain the things they needed to continue their work on the Quantum Tunnel. That meant turning toward some seedier elements of society.

And that meant Sonny Burch.

Burch was the lowest of the low as far as Hope was concerned. Her father and Sonny had crossed paths during Hank's S.H.I.E.L.D. days. "He's one of those people you don't want to know," she remembered Hank saying. "But one day, you might need to."

He was as shifty and shady as they came. In plain terms, Sonny was a fence—someone who deals in stolen goods. He bought stolen stuff from people at a low price, then sold it to others at a substantial markup. Rumor had it that Sonny used to fence stuff for Hydra, the same organization that S.H.I.E.L.D. had fought against for years.

Another rumor was that Sonny was a stone-cold killer.

All of this made Hope decidedly uncomfortable. She could take care of herself, sure, but she worried about her father. And she worried that having anything to do with Sonny might jeopardize the important work they were doing to try to reach the Quantum Realm and rescue Hope's mom.

As if sensing her internal struggle, Hank turned to Hope and said, "I know what Sonny is. But I also know it's the only way to get the parts we need to make the Quantum Tunnel a reality."

Hope nodded. "I know," she said. "I just don't want him to screw up anything."

The van pulled up in front of a battered-looking diner with one broken, boarded-up window. Hope took a deep breath, full of anger that everything had come to this.

"If Sonny tries anything, we'll be ready," Hank said. "We know who we're dealing with."

Hope got out of the van without saying another word and closed the door.

The diner was grimy and grubby, and the floor looked as if it hadn't been scrubbed in about twenty years, give or take. As Hope strode past the counter, the woman standing behind the register didn't even bother to look up. She was busy putting a roll of pennies into the till, squinting at her hands.

"Sit anywhere you want," the woman said, sounding grouchy and tired. "Not like we got a lot of business," she muttered under her breath.

Hope didn't say a word, simply nodded and continued past the counter, noticing just how empty the diner was. Aside from an old guy eating a bowl of soup (more like dribbling soup all over his beard), there was no one else there.

Except in the booth all the way in back.

That's where Hope saw Sonny Burch waiting for her. As usual, he had a couple of thugs, hired muscle there to protect Sonny in case anything went wrong. That, or they were there in case Sonny *wanted* something to go wrong.

"Pleasure to see you again," Sonny said, motioning with his right hand for Hope to have a seat.

Hope remained standing.

"I've got the money," Hope said, wanting this to be over with quickly. "Do you have the part?"

Sonny leaned back in his seat and took a small sip from a mug. "Worst coffee in the state," he said, pointing at the mug. "I come here to be reminded that I like the finer things in life."

Funny, I was thinking the same thing, Hope thought.

"The part?" Hope asked again.

Sonny took another sip of coffee. "I see you get right down to business. I like that. Well, maybe I have the part, and maybe I don't. Let's see what you got first."

Hope's eyes darted back and forth, checking to see if anyone was looking. There was still only the old guy eating/wearing his soup, and the woman behind the counter, who had moved on to making coffee. Satisfied that no one was watching, Hope removed an envelope from her pocket and placed it on the table.

"It's all there," Hope said, "as agreed."

One of the thugs seated to Sonny's left reached for the envelope, and Sonny shot him a withering glance. "Did I tell you to take the envelope?" he asked, in the tone a parent might use with a child who had just disobeyed.

The thug shrugged his shoulders.

"Good help is hard to find," Sonny said as he reached out to grab the envelope.

Then Hope slammed her right hand down on top of Sonny's.

Hard.

The thugs were up in a flash, hands digging into their coats, obviously reaching for their weapons.

"The part," Hope said flatly.

Sonny looked at Hope, staring her in the eyes, as if he were testing her resolve. He smiled in approval as her gaze told him she wasn't going to back down. Without breaking eye contact, he said, "Easy, easy. She just wants to make sure everything's fair and square." With that, he nodded toward his thugs, who pulled their hands from their jackets and sat back down at the table.

Then Sonny pulled a small envelope from his own jacket. He slid the envelope over to Hope.

"Take a look," he said. "As promised. Now, my money?"

Hope took the envelope and lifted her right hand, releasing Sonny and the envelope containing the money.

Checking inside her envelope, Hope found a small vial containing a very small computer chip.

"Exactly the one you wanted," Sonny said as he started to count the money Hope had given to him. "Sorry if it's not your color." His tone was patronizing. Hope gritted her teeth to stop something coming out of her mouth that she might regret—Sonny was deplorable, but right now he was her and Hank's only means of continuing their work. Hope cursed Scott all over again for putting them in this unfortunate position.

Hope clasped the vial tightly in her hand and forced a placid smile. "It's all there," she said.

"It better be," Sonny said, grinning back. "Pleasure doing business with you. See you again soon."

CHAPTER ELEVEN

Daddy, your foot is blinking!" Cassie said, pointing a finger at Scott's foot.

"You want my foot?" Scott asked. He was sitting on the floor with his daughter, and they were in the middle of building a massive fort. The two had gathered every cushion, every pillow, every blanket, every chair they could find in the house, and constructed an impressive stronghold.

"Not your foot. The bracelet," Cassie said, squirming like a snake through a pillow-lined tunnel. "It's blinking. I like it. Do you think Mom would let me get one, too?"

"How in the—?" Scott said, angling a sofa cushion in front of a tunnel. Cassie was right. Out of nowhere, Scott's ankle monitor had gone off. But how? He hadn't left the house. He hadn't even so much as set one foot outside the front door. Of all the lousy times for the ankle monitor to go on the blink, right when he was having a blast with Cassie.

It figures, Scott thought. *Even when I follow the rules and don't do anything, something has to go wrong.*

"Let's hold the pillow fort for a minute," Scott said. "I have to make a quick call." He needed to call Agent Woo right away if he was going to prevent another house visit from the feds. The last thing he wanted on his record was another "incident," like the newspaper thing. Like he was ever going to live that one down.

He wanted to let Woo know in no uncertain terms that he hadn't done anything to violate the terms of his agreement. Not that Woo would necessarily believe him, at least, not right away. But Scott had to do something. He couldn't risk being taken back to prison and losing Cassie.

Not again.

"Daddy, watch out!" Cassie called out. "If you get up now, you'll—"

As Scott got up from the floor without thinking, he first took a big blanket with him. The blanket then took out the pillows holding it in place along the top of the fort. Then the cushion walls collapsed. In a hot second, he had destroyed the pillow fort like some rampaging monster. Scott surveyed his handiwork, shaking his head.

Then Cassie let out a loud whoop. "Do it again!" she said.

"Have you seen my phone?" Scott asked Cassie.

She shrugged her shoulders. "No. Maybe you left it in the kitchen?"

"Good thinking, Peanut," Scott said, and he raced out of the room, feeling as if every second that passed was drawing the feds closer and closer to his house, to his daughter. Scott ran down the stairs to the kitchen. Maybe he had left it on the counter while he was making sandwiches for Cassie and himself. No sooner had he set foot in the kitchen, than he ran smack into Luis.

"Scotty, I been thinking, about the business—" Luis started.

Scott placed the palm of his right hand on Luis's chest. "Not right now, Luis. I gotta find my phone and make a call right away, before—"

"It'll just take a second," Luis continued. "You know how we need to get that business plan together to show to that guy who wants to hire us to do his security? Well, I think we have to do it sooner rather than later, or we're gonna miss out on the—"

"Yeah, I got that, Luis, but if I don't find my phone, there's gonna be—"

"Right, there's gonna be a chance that we lose the gig, and we don't want to do that. So I've been thinking, that we just need you to put together the final presentation that will sell us to this dude. So what do you—"

Suddenly, there was a knock at the front door. A steady, polite, insistent knock.

"Unbelievable," Scott said, knowing full well what was going to happen next.

CHAPTER TWELVE

A surprise visit from Jimmy Woo," Scott said, trying to keep the sarcasm out of his voice as he opened the front door. Agent Woo was wearing a black suit, his short hair swept back on his head. The federal agent wasn't smiling, but he wasn't frowning, either. He was just sort of...expressionless. Scott wondered what that meant.

"Hello, Scott," Woo said, his voice surprisingly friendly. "We were in the neighborhood, when we saw that you were having a little problem." Woo pointed at the monitor on Scott's ankle. It continued to flash.

"About that, look, I wasn't doing anything," Scott protested. "I was just building a massive pillow fort *inside* my house, and—"

"Oh, is Cassie here?" Woo asked. "Mind if I come in for a moment?"

Scott sighed, then gestured for Woo to come in. He saw there were at least two other agents standing outside the front door. Woo motioned for them to stay there while he went inside. Scott closed the door.

"Like I was saying, I wasn't doing anything," Scott

said. He was frustrated and angry. Mostly, he was mad at himself for being in this situation in the first place. "This isn't like the newspaper thing."

"Relax, Scott, I believe you," Woo said, his voice cool and calm.

"Wait…you do?" Scott asked, suspicious, waiting for the other shoe to drop.

"Yes. We can tell if you actually left the premises at all, and we know you didn't go anywhere. I see that you're here now. Clearly you were inside when we came, and the way that monitor is flashing indicates that there's been a minor malfunction. We'll have a replacement monitor brought inside in just a few minutes," Woo said.

Scott's shoulders slumped, and he exhaled in relief. "Thank you," he said.

"Sure," Woo said. "See? Nothing like the newspaper incident at all. You know, everyone back at the home office still talks about that one." Woo let out a short guffaw and clapped Scott on the back.

"That's great," Scott said halfheartedly.

"You're a funny guy," Woo replied. He stood there in the downstairs room, looking around. Scott could tell that he wasn't just looking to look. He seemed to be searching for signs of something. But what?

"Agent Woo?" Cassie called from the top of the stairs.

"Hey, there she is!" Woo said, pointing at Cassie, who trotted down the stairs and came to stand beside Scott.

"You're not going to take him away, are you?" Cassie asked. Her face scrunched up, and she scowled at Agent Woo.

"Nope, not at all," Agent Woo said. "We're here to help your dad with his ankle monitor, since there seems to be a problem. But seeing as how I'm already here…"

"Did you hear that?" Scott asked.

"I didn't hear anything," Agent Woo said.

"Me either," Cassie added.

"It was the sound of the other shoe dropping," Scott said.

Agent Woo chuckled. "Good one. Listen, since I'm already here, I wanted to just remind you of a little something, Scott. The terms of your"—he paused to correct himself—"*our* agreement."

"I'm following each and every one," Scott said. "I'm clean."

"Oh, I know," Woo said as he walked around the room slowly, still looking. "It's just I find it's helpful to offer little reminders every now and then. Like the part about having any contact with former associates who have been or are currently in violation of the Sokovia Accords or any related statutes—"

"I haven't seen, heard, talked to, IM'd, tin-canned anybody," Scott said, growing more and more confused. *Where is this coming from?* he wondered.

"Not saying you did. Just wanted to make sure you understood that doing so carries with it a pretty steep penalty. A twenty-year penalty, to be precise," Agent Woo said, his voice suddenly serious.

Twenty years. That meant if he had any contact with Hope or Hank, and Agent Woo found out about it, that Scott would be sent back to prison for twenty years. Twenty more years missing from the life he should have with Cassie, watching his daughter grow up. Scott tried to calm himself down. *That is not going to happen.*

The front door opened and another black-suited agent walked in, carrying a small cardboard box. The agent handed the box to Woo, then turned around and left, closing the door behind her.

"Your new ankle monitor," Agent Woo said, removing the plastic object from the box. "Let's have a look." He knelt down and pressed a series of buttons that released the ankle monitor. Woo took the monitor off Scott's ankle, then attached the new one. He pressed another series of buttons, and the ankle monitor tightened around Scott.

"Ow," Scott said sharply.

"Sorry," Agent Woo said. "Too tight?"

"Yeah, a little," Scott said, rubbing his ankle.

"Well, it has to be. Don't want it coming off by accident," Agent Woo said. Standing up, he smiled at Scott. "I'm glad we had the chance to reconnect," he said. "Remember what we talked about. If anyone reaches out to you, calls you, stops by, whatever—you let us know right away."

"Understood," Scott said. "You'll be the first to know. Oh, and Agent Woo?"

The federal agent looked at Scott, raising his eyebrows in acknowledgment.

"Were you . . . looking for anything particular? Or do you just really like what we've done with the place?" Scott asked sarcastically.

Agent Woo grinned and turned his gaze to the front door. "Looking to see if anything was out of place, if something didn't match up with your story," he said. "You're clean."

"Wow, you can tell all that just by looking around the living room?" Scott asked playfully.

"If you were lying, we'd know about it," Agent Woo said. "Trust me."

"I have no doubt," Scott replied.

With that, Agent Woo smiled at Cassie, shook Scott's hand, and headed to the front door. Scott opened it, watched Woo leave, and then slammed it shut.

"He's weird," Cassie said, staring after him.

"Well, he works for the government," Scott replied.

CHAPTER THIRTEEN

What have you done, Hank?

That's the thought that was careening through Scott's mind at the moment. There was no doubt that the people from Pym Technologies whom Luis had been talking about earlier were Hank and Hope. They just had to be, Scott knew it. Just as there was also no doubt that Jimmy Woo had come over to his house not just about the ankle monitor, but to deliver a clear warning: Stay away from Hank Pym and Hope Van Dyne. The timing between Luis's monologue and Woo's little surprise visit was too much of a coincidence—whatever Luis had heard through the grapevine, the feds must be onto as well.

So what is Hank up to? Scott wondered.

"Daddy, can you help me with my homework?"

Cassie's voice jolted Scott out of his reverie. "Yes, of course, your homework!" he said. "I didn't even realize you had homework that you needed to do. You should have told me earlier, Cassie." He glanced at the wall clock nervously. If Cassie's mom came to pick her up and found her homework left undone, it would be yet another black mark against Scott.

"I forgot, but now I remembered," Cassie said, as if that were a perfectly reasonable explanation.

Scott sighed. "Well, what do you have to do, Peanut?" he asked. His thoughts surrounding Jimmy Woo's visit were still bouncing around in his head, and Scott was having a little trouble focusing. *This must be what Luis feels like all the time,* he thought.

"I need to write about what I want to be when I grow up," she said.

Scott brightened for a second. "That's a pretty cool thing to write about," he said, smiling at Cassie. "Any ideas what you want to be? I mean, it's a big world; you can do anything you want."

"Oh, I already know!" Cassie said, leaping up and down.

Laughing, Scott said, "And what's that?"

"I want to be Ant-Man!" she said, full of enthusiasm.

"Ant-Man?" Scott said, genuinely surprised. "Why do you want to be Ant-Man?"

"Because *you're* Ant-Man! And I love you and you're awesome and you're the best and I want to be Ant-Man," Cassie rambled.

"I know, but Ant-Man's our secret, right?" Scott said, looking into Cassie's eyes.

The girl smiled back and said, "I know. It would just be really cool to shrink and do stuff. But that's okay because I have something else I want to be when I grow up. "

"What's that?" Scott asked, taking the bait.

"I want to run an ice-cream store!" Cassie shouted. "Just like you used to do!"

"Running your own ice-cream store would be awesome," Scott said, marveling at how Cassie could zoom between ideas so quickly.

"Yes!" Cassie shouted. "Because ice cream is the best, and working at an ice-cream place is, like, my dream!"

Scott laughed, and realized that, to a kid, working in an ice-cream place probably *would* seem like a dream job.

"Working at an ice-cream place is everyone's dream job," Luis said, popping into the room.

"Where did you go, Luis?" Scott asked. "You were here one minute; then Agent Woo showed up and *POOF!* Gone."

Luis flashed a brief smile and blinked. "Oh, I get

nervous around that dude. He's kinda weird, you know what I'm sayin'?"

"That's what I was saying!" Cassie shouted. The pair high-fived again.

"So smart," Luis said, mussing Cassie's hair. "Anyway, Scotty, I talked to that dude who knows the dude who works for the dude, and I got some info for you."

"Let me make one quick call, and then I'm all yours, Cassie," Scott said. "I'll tell you all the ice-cream secrets I know."

"Oooooooh," Cassie said as she ran to grab her homework folder out of her backpack.

Scott left the room and headed into the kitchen for a little privacy. Except...Luis was sitting at the table, staring at him.

"You're really gonna sit here while I call him, aren't you?" Scott asked.

"I won't say anything. I just want to be here when you talk to him," Luis said. "It's so cool."

Scott sighed, then dialed the number. The phone rang once, and then someone picked up.

"Aren't you not supposed to be talking to me?" the

voice on the other end of the phone said. Scott thought he sounded annoyed.

"Technically? Not at all," he replied. "But I really need a favor, and you know I can't leave the house, and I can't use e-mail, and—"

"You don't have my e-mail," Sam Wilson said. There was silence from Scott on the other end. "You *don't* have my e-mail, do you?"

"No, I just have this number. Look, I wouldn't even be calling unless it was important, you know that," Scott said, trying to make his case.

"I'd like to help you, Tic Tac," Sam offered. "But we're kind of in the middle of it here."

"It's just a background check. Take you two minutes," Scott said. "Maybe even one, because everyone knows that Falcon has, like, mad computer skills."

"Do they now?"

"Yeah," Scott said, making it up as he went along. "That's the word on the street."

"Uh-huh," Sam said skeptically. "Tell you what. Cap's got something cooking, but we *might* have a little down time. You give me the information, and I'll see what I can do."

"Thanks, Sam, I really appreciate it," Scott said, trying not to sound too hopeful.

"Don't get your hopes up," Sam replied.

I sounded too hopeful, Scott thought. *What a moron.*

"The guy's name is Sonny," Scott began. "He's a bad guy, a fence. Deals in stolen merchandise, but really high-tech stuff. He had contact with a couple of people from Pym Technologies in the last couple weeks. I want to know more about him."

There was silence on the other end of the phone.

"You get all that, Sam?" Scott asked.

" 'The guy's name is *Sonny*? That's all you got?' " Sam said. "And just like that, I'm supposed to find out about this guy?' "

"You're an Avenger."

"Ex-Avenger," Sam corrected. "All right, let me see what I can do."

"Thanks, Sam," Scott said as he hung up the phone.

"Sooooo?" Luis said, the vowel long and drawn-out. "Did he ask about me?"

CHAPTER FOURTEEN

H ope was still trying to get used to their new place. It was even bigger than the lab they had been working out of in Hank's house; that was for sure. And there was an even more impressive array of equipment. They had been making real progress on the Quantum Tunnel. And with the new part that Hope had just brought in, they would officially be one step closer to finding her mother.

"Here's the part," Hope said, handing the small vial to Hank.

"Great," Hank answered, not looking up from his workbench. He was wearing a welding mask atop his head and had an acetylene torch in his right hand. "You can give it to our friend *Odontomachus* there," he said, putting the mask down and igniting the torch.

Hope looked over shoulder to see a large *Odontomachus bauri*—a trap-jaw ant—come walking toward her. Only this wasn't a tiny ant. Thanks to the Pym Particles, this trap-jaw ant was the size of a large dog, maybe bigger. For a while now, Hank had been having some enlarged trap-jaw ants helping out in the laboratory, providing another pair of hands—pincers, really—when needed. Without saying a word, she handed the vial over to the trap-jaw ant. The insect opened its mandibles and gently took the vial from her. Then the ant walked away with the vial and placed it carefully in a foam-lined case.

Amazing, Hope thought. *That thing could crush someone's bones with those jaws, and yet, here it is, carrying that vial as carefully as if it were a baby.*

She watched as the trap-jaw ant ambled on. Then she turned her attention back to Hank, who was busy welding some new component together. She waited until he was done and had pulled the mask off.

"He knows we're working on something, and he's going to want a piece of it," Hope said. "The longer we keep this relationship up, the more dangerous it's going to be to pull out."

Hank didn't say anything, seemingly staring off into space.

"Dad. Are you listening to me?" Hope asked, her tone impatient.

"It won't be long now," Hank said. "We're getting there, Hope. For the first time, I really feel like we're making progress. We should have been done with this sooner, but…I think there's light at the end of the tunnel." His mouth quirked upward as he finished his sentence.

Hope smiled at Hank's little joke, but she also felt it. And then there was the part of her, the practical part, asking, *Okay, so let's say you do get the Quantum Tunnel working. Then what? How are you going to find my mother? Where do you even start?*

And then the light seemed as if it were just a little further away.

"How?" Hope said softly.

"How what?" Hank asked.

She looked at the controls, at the panels, at the rudimentary tunnel that the two had been constructing. "How?" she said once more.

Hank stood up from the workbench and walked over to Hope, placing his hands on her shoulders. "I don't know," he answered. "Your mother could be anywhere. I know that finding a way into and out of the Quantum Realm is only part of the equation here. But it's the part we have to solve before we can even consider anything else."

"I know," Hope said. She swallowed and felt the lump in her throat. "But to come this far, to be so close... What if we go to the Quantum Realm and we just can't find her?"

"We will find your mother," Hank said.

"How do you know?" Hope asked.

But Hank didn't have an answer.

Hope and Hank had been working on the Quantum Tunnel for at least six hours since she returned from her meeting with Sonny Burch. Neither had eaten or taken a break. Since their conversation about trying to find Hope's mom in the Quantum Realm, they hadn't even exchanged a word. It was as though their mutually unspoken fears had propelled them to push even harder, even faster, to get their work done.

Hope looked over at Hank and saw that he had fallen asleep, slumped over in his chair. She picked up a blanket that was sitting on a chest behind him and draped it over his shoulders. Then she walked over to the door and out of the lab.

The air was cool and damp. The sky was dark. As she looked around, she saw nothing and no one. This time they'd set up their lab right on the beach, and Hope gazed off into the distance to see the ocean waves lapping at the sandy shore.

That's one plus to having a truly portable lab, Hope thought with irony. *Beachfront property whenever you want it. If you like that sort of thing. Which I don't.*

Walking along on the beach, she looked up at the sky, thinking back to the meeting with Sonny Burch at the diner earlier that day. She thought of Sonny's false grin, the goons he had surrounding him, the downtrodden woman behind the counter, the empty tables. And finally, she thought of the old guy sitting in the booth, eating his soup, spilling it all over his beard.

A sudden, terrible thought occurred to Hope. *What if that guy wasn't just some old man? What if he was a government agent? What if the woman behind the counter was* also *a government agent?*

How long did she and Hank have before their secret was out and they were apprehended, placed in government custody while their technology was auctioned off to the highest bidder? If that happened, the Quantum Tunnel would never be completed. And the already slim chance they had of locating and rescuing Hope's mom would be wiped out for good.

Then she thought about Scott. She still wanted to plaster one right across his face for all he'd done. But

Hope also couldn't deny that there was a part of her that wanted Scott to be there with them now. Because he could listen, be a sounding board in a way that Hank couldn't. Because... because why?

Because that big dummy can actually be helpful, she thought. *And because... I miss him.*

CHAPTER FIFTEEN

Scott looked away from Luis and stared at Cassie, who had wandered into the kitchen.

"Is he what now?" Scott asked.

Luis was quick to jump in. "Oh, good question, I get it. Like, is your bro Falcon part bird, or is he a bird who's part man, or—"

"He's a guy who wears mechanical wings," Scott said flatly. "Just a guy. Just a regular, ordinary guy."

Cassie looked down at the floor, disappointed. "It would have been cool if he was at least part bird," she muttered.

"Agreed," Luis said.

"Homework," Scott said, clapping his hands together. "Your mom is gonna be here in just a little bit. We should finish up that assignment so you're ready to go when she gets here." *And so I don't get yelled at,* he added silently.

Cassie pouted, her lower lip jutting out just a little. "If we do my homework really fast, will you tell me more about Falcon?"

"Okay, it's a deal," Scott said. "But no rushing through your homework. It's really important."

"Yeah, you want to get all the details on that ice-cream job," Luis added. "Like, do you get paid in ice cream?"

Scott stared at him, shaking his head.

When Scott and Sam Wilson had first met, Scott had still been AMIT—Ant-Man-In-Training.

"The final phase of your training will be a stealth incursion."

Hank Pym's voice was loud and clear in Scott's ears, even over the sound of the jet engines. He had to be, what, fifteen thousand feet off the ground? Maybe more? Clinging to the side of an airplane at tiny ant size, there was Scott, along with three squadrons of flying ants.

"It's freezing!" Scott shouted into the commlink. "You couldn't make a suit with flannel lining?"

The reason Scott was risking his life by hanging on to the side of an airplane was simple. He had to retrieve a device that he, Hank, and Hope would need if they were going to successfully sneak into Darren Cross's lab and steal the Yellowjacket suit. The device would help them override the building's security measures.

The tricky part was that the device was currently

stored away in an old storage facility in upstate New York that had belonged to Howard Stark. Hank thought that the mission was going to be . . . how had he put it? "A piece of cake." Get into the abandoned facility, get the device, get out. Easy-peasy.

And like the idiot he was, Scott had believed him.

When they got over the target area, Scott ordered the three squadrons of flying ants to take flight. Then he hopped on the back of his own steed, a flying ant who he had taken to calling Ant-thony.

"All right, Ant-thony, please don't drop me this time!" he pleaded, holding on for dear life, as he and Ant-thony flew through the sky alongside the other ants.

They descended through the clouds, coming up on the facility's coordinates. Only Scott noticed something was wrong the second he made visual contact. On the roof of the facility, plain as day, was a big *A* symbol.

A for *Avengers*.

It may have been a Howard Stark facility at some point, but now it belonged to Tony Stark's team of Super Heroes.

So much for "a piece of cake."

"Scott, get out of there!" Hope shouted over the commlink. Via miniaturized cameras mounted on the ants, she and Hank could see everything that was happening from the safety of Hank's home.

"Abort! Abort now!" Hank hollered.

"No, it's okay," Scott said as Ant-thony swooped in for a closer look. "It doesn't look like anyone's home. Ant-thony, get me to the roof!"

Moments later, Scott jumped off Ant-thony's back and landed on the roof, tucking his chin. He rolled to his feet, surveying his surroundings.

"All right, I'm on the roof of the target building," he said into the commlink. He was a little out of breath, but everything was going to be fine.

"Somebody's home, Scott," said Hope.

Or not.

Scott looked up, only to see Falcon himself flying in from above and landing on the roof.

"What's going on down there, Sam?" came a voice over Falcon's wrist communicator.

"I had a sensor trip," Sam said, looking around the rooftop. "But I'm not seeing anything. Wait a second..."

Again, Hank screamed into the commlink, "Abort, Scott! Abort now!"

"It's okay, he can't see me," Scott replied. He was confident that at his tiny size, there was absolutely no way that Falcon would ever notice him. All Scott had to do now was lie low and wait for the Avenger to leave.

"I can see you," Falcon said.

"He can see me," Scott muttered. He stared at Falcon for a second and noted the goggles he wore that must have had some kind of macro/micro vision embedded.

Pressing the button on his left hand, Scott suddenly sprang up to his normal height. He hit a button on the side of his helmet, and his faceplate rose to reveal his features. "Hi," he said brightly. "I'm Scott."

Falcon looked unmoved. "What are you doing here?" he asked flatly, sizing up Scott.

Scott hadn't expected running into anyone, let alone an Avenger, on his very first field mission. He was a little starstruck. "First off, I'm a big fan," Scott said.

"Appreciate it. So who are you?" Falcon pressed.

In that moment, Scott had tried to stand as tall and proud as he could. In his most heroic voice he said, "I'm Ant-Man."

He regretted it the second it came out of his mouth.

"Ant-Man?" Falcon asked, unable to fight back the smile creeping up on his face.

"What, you haven't heard of me?" Scott stumbled. "No, you wouldn't have heard of me."

"You wanna tell me what you want?"

Scott forged onward, despite his botched introduction. "I was hoping I could grab a piece of technology, just for a few days. I'm gonna return it—I need it to save the world. You know how that is." Scott rushed his words, really, really hoping that Falcon would know how it was.

"I know exactly how that is," Falcon said, and then he started to walk toward Scott with purpose. He raised his right arm and spoke into his wrist communicator. "Located the breach," he said. "Bringing him in."

CHAPTER SIXTEEN

S orry about this!" Scott shouted, pressing the button on his right glove. As Falcon tried to grab him, Scott shrank out of sight. He felt bad. After all, Falcon was one of the good guys. And wasn't Ant-Man one of the good guys, too?

He *was* one of the good guys...wasn't he?

There was no time to think about that. Scott jumped off the roof, aiming right for Falcon's chin. He staggered the Avenger with an unexpected punch. Falcon activated his flight pack and took off. The wind generated by his wings sent Scott tumbling off the roof.

"What are you doing?!" Hank shouted over the commlink. Scott knew that Hank was watching everything. And clearly getting angrier and angrier as each minute ticked by.

Scott caught a lucky break. The wind was with him, and he drifted to the ground rather than falling outright. When he landed, he took off into a sprint. Overhead, he could see Falcon adjusting something on the side of his goggles—no doubt watching every move "Ant-Man" made.

"Breach is an adult male, who has some sort of shrinking tech," he heard Falcon say into his wrist communicator.

Some sort of shrinking tech, Scott thought. *Yeah, you could say that.*

As Scott ran, Falcon swooped down toward him. Quickly deactivating his flight pack, Falcon landed on the ground. To Scott's surprise, the Avenger actually tried to step on him! Scott turned and rolled to avoid the massive foot that threatened to crush him. Then he leaped up and punched Falcon twice. Even when Ant-Man was in his shrunken state, his punches packed the wallop of a full-size person, all concentrated into one small spot.

Falcon wasn't having it. He activated the flight pack again and flew backward. Grabbing two weapons, he immediately opened fire at the area where he thought Scott was.

Only Scott wasn't there.

Instead, he was perched atop one of Falcon's weapons, holding on for dear life as vibrations the weapons were giving off threatened to dislodge him.

Then Scott punched Falcon twice more and disarmed the winged hero.

Enlarging to his regular size, Scott tried to land

another blow. Only Falcon was ready. He caught Scott and got in a couple of punches of his own.

Scott didn't like that part very much.

"That's enough!" Falcon shouted. He took off into the air, holding on to Scott, pummeling him again. But before he could get in another punch, Scott managed to slam the button on his right hand. Once again, he shrank and seemingly disappeared.

Momentarily dazed, Falcon looked around for any sign of the tiny invader. That's when Scott enlarged again and jumped right on Falcon's shoulders! He wrapped his legs around Falcon's neck like a pair of scissors, and the two fell back onto the ground. There was a brief struggle before Falcon hit the controls on his flight pack. Suddenly, the two men scooted along the ground backward. They slid across the grass, Falcon punching at Scott.

Scott fumbled with the controls on his glove. Tired of getting hit by an Avenger, Scott managed to slam down the right button, and he shrank. Unbalanced, Falcon flipped over, landing on his back.

This is getting me nowhere, Scott thought. *I can stay here and fight Falcon all day, or I can grab what I came here for and get away as soon as possible.*

Sprinting along the grass, Scott headed back toward the storage facility. Enlarging himself, Scott immediately felt a sharp blow across the back of his neck. On his way down to the ground once again, he saw Falcon behind him.

Scott managed to shrink, and this time he called for backup. "Ant-thony," he said, "a little help!"

No sooner had he spoken the words than the flying ant zoomed up alongside Scott. He ran and jumped onto Ant-thony's back, and the two headed for the storage facility.

The facility was shut tight as a drum, the huge metal door closed. That would keep out any normal-size thief. But not Ant-Man. There were a few slots in the door for ventilation purposes. Very small, but they seemed positively cavernous to Scott and his flying steed. Together, they flew straight toward one of the tiny vents and entered the darkened room.

A second or two later, the door rose up, and Falcon entered, looking for Scott. Then the door closed behind him.

The easy part had been grabbing the device for Hank. Scott had found it literally the second he and Ant-thony got inside the facility. The hard part now was deciding what to do about Falcon. Scott was tired of fighting, but also afraid that he would be caught, and *that* would be the end of his mission. Then Hank wouldn't get the part he needed, and Darren Cross would carry out his plans. And Scott would be a failure. Again.

So instead of doing what Ant-thony was now silently screaming for him to do—*leave!*—he headed straight for Falcon. And at his still-tiny size, he was able to jump in between a couple of the armored plates the hero wore, and work his way into the Avenger's flight pack.

It was dark inside, but Scott could make out a mess of wires and connections. He had no idea what they did specifically. But he figured if he pulled enough of them, Falcon would have trouble flying.

And sure enough, he was right. Without warning, Falcon shot backward, punching a hole in the metal door of the storage facility as he twirled around uncontrollably.

"He's inside my pack!" Falcon shouted. He was grabbing at his armor, trying to pull something off to get at his tiny assailant. It was too late.

"Sorry!" Scott shouted, once again feeling bad. "You seem like a really great guy!"

Falcon hit the ground, his flight pack rendered useless. Climbing to his feet, he hit the side of his goggles, magnifying his vision. Glancing around, he saw no sign of Ant-Man anywhere.

That's probably because, at that very moment, Scott was climbing out of Falcon's flight pack. A quick communication, and Ant-thony buzzed right by Falcon, unnoticed. Scott jumped onto the flying ant's back, and he was gone, device in hand, leaving behind a very dazed—and very angry—Avenger.

As he and Ant-thony flew away, Scott could have sworn he heard Falcon mutter over his radio, "It's really important to me that Cap never finds out about this."

CHAPTER SEVENTEEN

Nice night for a walk," came a voice from behind her. "Isn't it, miss?"

Hope startled, practically jumping at the sound of the unexpected voice. She looked over her shoulder and saw a man approaching her on the beach. He was dressed in somewhat ratty-looking clothes, wearing an oversize hat with a floppy brim. He carried a metal detector in his right hand, and he waved it back and forth over the surface of the sand.

"Yes, it is," Hope answered, lying. Ever since she was a little girl, she had always disliked going to the beach. She took a breath, trying to calm herself. To say she was on edge after the meeting with Sonny Burch was putting it mildly.

"Well, I see the moon's coming out. What's the old saying? 'Moon is bright, sailor take flight?' Something like that?" The man smiled, his demeanor friendly and open.

Hope laughed. "I have no idea. I only know the one about, 'red sky in the morning, sailors take warning,'" she said.

The man chuckled. "Well, anyway, they're all just old

wives' tales, Hope. What brings you out to the beach tonight?" he asked.

Hope wrapped her arms around herself tightly. The wind felt a little cool, but that wasn't the only reason for the sudden chill that was running up her spine.

The man had called her Hope.

Something was desperately wrong.

"How did you know my name?" Hope asked the man. She dropped her arms to her sides, her hands instinctively curling up into fists.

The man smiled and laughed once more, his tone even and unhurried. "I think you misheard me. I just said that I hope it's an old wives' tale. So do you—"

Before the man could say another word, Hope crouched down and swept out her right leg. She tripped the man, who spiraled into the air for a brief moment before hitting the sand on his back. Moving fast, Hope planted her left foot on the man's abdomen, knocking the wind out of him. The man gasped for breath as he lay faceup on the sand, helpless.

"How did you know my name?" Hope asked again, each word measured. She kept her foot on the man's chest, slowly moving it up toward his throat. The man caught his breath.

"Okay, okay," he said, still gasping. "I was there. Today. At the diner."

Hope had a flash of recognition. The old man with the beard. Of course. She should have trusted her intuition from the get-go that something wasn't right about him and followed up on it before leaving the diner. Now he'd found out her and Hank's hiding place and could cause all sorts of trouble for them. *Sloppy, Hope, so sloppy,* she scolded herself.

"Who do you work for?"

The man remained silent, averting his gaze. Hope applied a little pressure to the man's larynx with her foot. He spasmed briefly, then waved his arms wildly in surrender. Hope eased off his throat slightly.

"You were saying?"

"We've been looking for you, Hope. You and your father. The work you're doing. The people I represent... We could make it worth your while. You wouldn't have to run anymore," the man said, struggling to get the words out.

"What. People," Hope spat out through gritted teeth.

"Some old friends of your father's, let's say," the man said.

"S.H.I.E.L.D.?" she asked.

The man shook his head. "There's no S.H.I.E.L.D. anymore, not like your father remembers. Let's just say that these people are aware of your difficulties, and they're prepared to make things a bit easier for you with the authorities...."

The man continued to speak, his voice picking up steam now that he'd gotten to make his pitch, but the words became a kind of dull roar in Hope's ears, as vague as the sound of the ocean's crashing waves in the distance. This whole situation unnerved her. And what she liked least right now was how quickly and easily the man was giving up information. Something else was wrong.

She didn't know why, but Hope suddenly felt the urge to run.

The man was still talking when Hope kicked him in the face, knocking him out. Then she ran across the beach as fast as she could. From the corner of her eye, she could have sworn she saw a car's headlights turn on in the distance and begin to move.

Hope ran faster.

CHAPTER EIGHTEEN

We need to move," Hope said as she threw open the door to the mobile laboratory. She slammed the door shut behind her. "Now," she added for emphasis.

Hope's sense of urgency seemed to be lost on Hank. He was busy at the controls of what was slowly but surely becoming the Quantum Tunnel. Hope noticed that he was holding the small vial she had obtained from Sonny Burch earlier that day. Gently, he removed the cap on the vial. Then, with a pair of tweezers, he reached inside, pulling out the tiny chip, his gray eyebrows furrowed in concentration.

Staring at her father incredulously, Hope repeated: "Dad, did you hear a word I said? We need. To move. Now."

"I heard you the first time," Hank said out of the side of his mouth, still laser-focused on the task before him. "I'm in the middle of something...delicate."

Impatient, Hope watched as Hank manipulated the chip with the tweezers and placed it inside the control panel. It looked as if Hank weren't even breathing. His movements were controlled, precise. At last, he removed the tweezers and took a deep, long breath.

"Okay. Now what's this about moving?" Hank said.

"On the beach," Hope said. "Someone's after us."

"After us?" Hank said, agitated. "Who?"

"I'm not sure," Hope said. "The man said he knows you from your S.H.I.E.L.D. days. They want the Quantum Tunnel tech. They know about it. I don't know how, but they know."

A dog-size trap-jaw ant trotted past, taking the empty vial from Hank's hands with its mandibles and walking away.

"When I met Sonny Burch," Hope started, trying to slow down her voice, "there were two people in the diner. One behind the counter, and one seated at a table. I thought there was something off about them, but I couldn't put my finger on it. Now I have to wonder if they were agents, operatives, whatever. Watching me. Following me back here." She slammed her hand against the wall in frustration. "I should have neutralized the threat before leaving," she said angrily. "I'm sorry, Dad."

There was a brief moment of silence, interrupted by the chittering from the trap-jaw ant, who still held the vial in its mandibles.

"No, just put it back in the case, 325," Hank said. He didn't need to speak to the ant in order to communicate with it—the device he wore over his right ear took care of that. Hope thought that Hank had become accustomed to speaking out loud to the ants to relieve some of the loneliness of working long hours in the lab.

Hank looked at his daughter's guilt-ridden face. "Hope, Hope, come on now. It's all right," Hank said, his voice soft. "It's not your fault. Let's secure everything, shrink it down, and get out of here."

Outside the lab, Hope took in a lungful of the cool, salt-tinged air, hoping it would still her nerves. She peered around cautiously. She didn't see any sign of the phantom car from earlier. The ocean waves were lapping the beach.

"Hurry up," Hope called back to her father.

"I'm going as fast as I can," Hank said. "Need to make sure everything's set right before we reduce it to handheld size."

Hank then applied the Pym Particles to the laboratory, and the building miraculously began to shrink. Only a few seconds later, the lab was a mere fraction of its former size, resembling a small, portable cube. Hank pulled the handle up, grabbing the lab.

"Good to go," Hank said.

They ran up the beach and entered a secluded parking lot, moving past a sign that read BEACH CLOSED. They had picked this spot precisely because that section of the beach had been shut down for cleanup, which meant fewer prying eyes. Their van was waiting in a deserted corner of the lot.

"We'll take it from here, Dr. Pym" came a voice from the darkness.

Hope and Hank stopped short in their tracks. "Who's that?" Hank asked.

"Never mind who," the disembodied voice said. "Just give us the box."

Hope saw him first. The man stepped out of the shadows. It was the man with the metal detector who she'd knocked out—or thought she'd knocked out. Only he wasn't holding a metal detector anymore. He was holding a weapon of some kind. It looked as if it could be a gun, but it wasn't any sort of gun she had ever seen before.

"You," he said, pointing his weapon at Hope. "Move over there, away from the van."

"I think we better do as we're told," Hank whispered into Hope's ear. "For the moment."

Without saying a word, Hope moved away from the van and held her hands up. She moved slowly, making no sudden moves.

"Now you," the man with the weapon said, pointing at Hank. "Hand it over."

"Sure," Hank said. "Just let me set it down." As he placed it on the ground, Hank shot Hope a look. She knew that look all too well: *Be ready for anything.*

No sooner had Hank placed the portable lab down on the ground than it began to grow to its full size. The man with the weapon had obviously not expected that, and he jumped backward in surprise.

In that moment, Hope lunged forward and dove for the man's legs while Hank hit him from above. The weapon went flying out of the man's hand. It hit the ground about ten feet away, and discharged a beam of electricity into the night sky.

"I knew I hated the beach," Hope grumbled.

CHAPTER NINETEEN

The guy you're looking for is Sonny Burch," Sam Wilson's voice came through over the line, steady and assured.

"And just who is Sonny Burch? What do we have on him?" Scott asked. He was in the kitchen, holding the phone close to his ear, speaking in a low tone so his voice wouldn't carry. In the other room, Cassie was busy writing her homework assignment as Luis supervised. Scott knew that Cassie could finish the homework on her own—she was an excellent student. But he also knew that she liked to play, so Luis was there to help her stay focused on the assignment.

"He's got a rap sheet like you wouldn't believe," Sam replied. "Had some dealings with Hydra in the past, fencing stuff for them. He's a seriously bad dude. If you know someone who's mixed up with him, you better tell them to back off."

"Yeah, I figured," Scott said dully.

"And here's the other thing—not only is Burch a piece of work, but he's a wanted man. The feds would love to get their hands on him, and they're looking. So, anyone you know? They're gonna get caught in the cross fire."

"Yeah, I figured," Scott repeated. "Listen, Sam, thanks for this. I owe you one."

"You owe me, like, twenty," Sam said. "Look me up when you get out, Tic Tac."

Scott said good-bye and hung up the phone.

So there it was. Whatever Hope and Hank were up to, they were about to be caught between Sonny Burch and who-knows-what federal agency. And whatever they were working on, it was a safe bet that both the good guys and the bad guys would want it for their own purposes.

In this instance, it might even be difficult to tell the difference between the good guys and the bad guys altogether.

Scott stuck his head out of the kitchen and saw Luis lying on the floor, laughing. Cassie was nowhere to be found.

"Cassie?" he shouted. "Luis, where's Cassie? You're supposed to be helping her with her homework." He looked back at the kitchen table and saw her assignment, nearly done, but not quite.

"Yeah, I know. But she said she needed a break so she could clear her head, and then she had this awesome idea to play hide-and-seek," Luis said from the floor.

"And why are you on the floor for this?" Scott asked.

"Cassie put a great twist on the game. So, the person who's doing the seeking? They count to one hundred with their eyes closed, but they have to spin around in a circle while they do it while the other person hides," Luis said rapidly.

"And let me guess. You got mad dizzy and you fell down," Scott said.

"Yeah, I got mad dizzy and I fell down," Luis confirmed. "It's a great game."

Scott headed upstairs while Luis and Cassie played hide-and-seek. He should get Cassie back to the table and make her finish her homework assignment like a good dad would, but at the moment all he could think about was the information he'd gotten from Sam and what it meant. He was about to make a really stupid decision. And as usual when he made a really stupid decision, he wanted to be alone while doing it. That way, no one could talk him out of it.

He didn't really see a way around it. So much of what was happening to Hope and Hank was Scott's fault, really. If he hadn't agreed to help Captain America, and if he hadn't turned into a giant at the airport, and if he hadn't attracted so much attention to Hank Pym's shrinking tech, then maybe Hope and Hank wouldn't be in the situation they were in now.

So he thought that if he got his friends into this mess, the least he could do was to get them out of it. And maybe Scott Lang couldn't do that.

But Ant-Man could.

You're being an idiot, he said to himself as he walked up the stairs. *You do this, and you're going to risk everything—but mostly you're going to risk your relationship with your daughter. If you do this, dummy, you might not see Cassie again for a very, very long time.*

He reached the top of the stairs and opened the door to his room. He sat down on his bed and reached over to an adjacent shelf. There he found exactly what he was looking for. There was a small trophy with a plaque that read WORLD'S GREATEST GRANDMA. It had been a gift to him from Cassie. The day she went shopping, they were all out of WORLD'S GREATEST DAD trophies. So she picked this one out for him instead.

It was perfect. It summed up their shared sense of humor, and it had made them laugh like crazy.

But there was another reason why Scott wanted the trophy now. He picked it up and started to unscrew the base from the statue. When the base was open, he looked inside to find the miniaturized Ant-Man suit he had placed there.

He took a deep breath. *You ready to do this?* Scott thought. *Because if you are, then you better just—*

"Daddy! What are you doing in here?"

Scott fell off the bed and landed on the wood floor with a loud thud, the now-separate pieces of the trophy landing beside him.

"Ouch!"

"Don't tell Luis where I am!" Cassie said. Scott turned his head to the left, and looked under his bed. There was Cassie, hiding, a giant grin on her face and one finger pressed to her lips.

"Hide-and-seek, right," Scott said, slowly sitting up and rubbing the back of his head, brushing the trophy pieces out of view before Cassie could see them and ask questions. "Don't worry, Peanut. I won't say a word."

And you won't be putting on the Ant-Man suit, either, Scott thought. How could he have even considered it?

He could lose Cassie if he so much as left the house. Even if he found a way to deactivate the ankle monitor, or cheat it somehow, the risk was too great.

Scott stood up and screwed the base of the trophy back on, carefully placing it back on the shelf. He would have to find another way to help Hope and Hank.

CHAPTER TWENTY

Scott had an idea.

He reached for his cell phone only to realize it wasn't with him—he must have left it in the kitchen after his call with Sam. He bolted out of his room and ran down the stairs. He was taking two steps at a time, moving so fast that he didn't even see Luis before it was almost too late.

"Whoa, bro!" Luis said, affronted, as Scott very nearly collided into him. "You almost cratered both of us, and I'm in the middle of a game of hide-and-seek."

"Sorry," Scott managed to say as he hit the bottom of the stairs and took a sharp turn toward the kitchen—just as there was a knock at the front door.

Come on! Scott thought.

Scott jogged the few steps to the front door and opened it to find Maggie.

"Hi, Scott," Maggie said. "Cassie ready?"

"Maggie!" Scott said. "Cassie. Yes. I mean no. She's not ready—almost, though. She's playing a game of hide-and-seek with Luis. Come on in."

Maggie stepped inside the door and looked around. She saw the pillow fort aftermath on the floor, as well as Cassie's homework folder and assorted papers splayed out. She nodded slowly.

"Busy afternoon, huh?" Maggie asked.

"Oh yeah," Scott said. "About that. I mean, we were playing games, but we also did homework. Like, a lot of homework. So busy. There's still a little left, but—"

"That's okay, Scott," Maggie said. "Cassie comes here so you can have fun; she can finish her homework later. I'm glad you two had a good time together," Maggie said, smiling. "She loves you so much. These visits mean the world to her. You know that, Scott."

Scott felt his cheeks flush with embarrassment. The visits meant the world to him, too. And the fact that Cassie had waited to do her homework just to tell Scott that she wanted to be him when she grows up? He was ashamed that, even for a fraction of a second, he thought about doing anything that would jeopardize them.

"Yeah, they mean everything to me, too," Scott said. Then he turned toward the stairs and called up to Cassie.

"Big hugs, Daddy," Cassie said as she threw herself around Scott, wrapping her arms around his neck. She squeezed hard, and Scott squeezed back.

"Thanks for coming over, Peanut. I'll see you again next weekend, okay?" Scott said. "Let me know how the homework assignment goes."

"I will, promise," Cassie said, waving her folder. Then she looked at her mom. "Daddy told me all about working at the ice-cream store," she said. "*So* cool."

"I bet," Maggie said, rolling her eyes good-naturedly and winking at Scott. "I'll talk to you during the week," she said as she ushered Cassie out the front door. "Try not to get into any trouble."

"I'd walk you to the car, but I'm afraid I'd go off," Scott said, pointing to his ankle monitor. Maggie sighed, and she and Cassie headed to the car. Scott watched as they got in and drove off. He stood in the doorway, waving.

The second Maggie's car was out of sight, Scott ran into the kitchen and grabbed his phone. He speed-dialed a number, waiting anxiously as it rang.

"Agent Woo?" Scott said as the phone picked up.

"Scott Lang," Agent Woo answered. "Three in one

day. To what do I owe the honor? Anything I should know about?"

"Yeah, about that," Scott said. "I don't know if it's anything, but a friend of mine told me about a guy who's operating in the area, who might be after some material from Pym Technologies."

Scott swore he could actually hear Agent Woo's ears prick up at the mention of "Pym Technologies."

"I'm listening," Agent Woo said.

"The guy's name is Sonny Burch. Mean anything to you?"

There was quiet on the phone, and Scott heard some muttering, as if Woo had placed his hand over the receiver and was conferring with someone else. The muffling sound disappeared, and Woo's voice came back through clearly. "He's, erm, known to us. Do you know what he's after?"

Scott didn't know exactly what Burch wanted, but if it involved Hank and Hope, then he had a pretty good idea of what it was. "Not exactly," Scott said, fibbing. "I just heard the words *Pym Technologies*, and figured I should call you. I want to keep my nose clean, remember?"

"Of course you do," Agent Woo said. "You did the

right thing by calling us. And how did you come by this information? I don't have to remind you that if you were in contact with anyone from Pym Technologies, it would—"

"Violate the terms of our agreement, yes, I know," Scott said, trying not to sound annoyed, but failing. "Look, I haven't spoken with anyone from Pym Technologies—I already told you that. This came from a friend of mine. Through the security company we're trying to start up."

"Right, your security company," Woo said thoughtfully. "Well, thanks for the tip, Scott. We'll look into this Sonny Burch."

"Thanks," Scott said. "I appreciate it."

"No problem," Woo replied. "And, Scott?"

"Yeah?"

"Thank you. For being straight up about this. You're doing a good job, and we're all pulling for you," Woo said.

Scott couldn't believe it. Not the part about everyone pulling for him. Somehow, he had no trouble believing that. No, he couldn't believe that he was doing a good job, and that someone was actually recognizing it.

So much of his adult life, Scott had felt like a failure.

Failing Cassie by getting thrown into prison, not being there for her. Failing Maggie by not getting to be the father to Cassie and the husband to his wife that he'd intended to be. Failing himself, for all of the above.

Now it seemed as if he was finally picking up the pieces of his life and getting his act together.

He only hoped that nothing would happen to blow it.

CHAPTER TWENTY-ONE

Aren't you tired?" Hank asked. He was sitting in the passenger seat of their white van, head leaning against the cool window, yawning. Outside, it was dark. There were clouds in the sky, and the yellow light of the moon poked through only occasionally.

Hope was driving while her father tried to catch some sleep. They had been on the road for hours already. Paranoia gripped them both. They were afraid they were being followed, especially after the events back at the beach. So Hope kept on driving, taking back roads they never even knew existed and doubling back over their path sometimes before continuing onward.

"Not especially," Hope lied, trying to sound perky. Truth be told, she was exhausted. The adrenaline that had been shooting through her body since the incident at the beach was now wearing off, and she found her limbs feeling heavy. Her eyelids were weighing down, and Hope just wanted to close them, even for a minute. But she knew that her father had been pushing himself so hard working on the Quantum Tunnel, and that he needed the break more.

"Who do you think those guys were?" Hope asked.

"Could be anyone," Hank said. "Sonny Burch could have sent them. Could be some of the people that Cross had been in touch with before he disappeared. Splinter group of S.H.I.E.L.D., maybe Hydra. Maybe the CIA or FBI."

"So, basically, it could be anyone," Hope clarified. "We are so screwed."

"Yep," Hank said, nodding in agreement. "We are about as screwed as you get."

Hope had been thinking about it for a while, and wondered if she should broach the subject. She was sure that her father would hate the idea. Even she wasn't overly fond of it. There was still a king-size chip sitting on her shoulder.

"Scott," she said, trying out the word on her tongue, seeing how it sounded. It rang out loud and clear in the van's confined quarters. Hank didn't respond, so Hope tried again, the name coming easier this time. "Scott—"

But before another word or even another breath could get past her lips, Hank shut her down. "Stop," he said, and Hope felt as if she could almost hear his blood pressure rising. "Not another word about him. He's the reason for all of this. He's made a mess of everything. I don't want his help, and we don't need it."

"He's not my favorite person in the world, either," Hope said, agreeing with her father. "But we do need some kind of help. We can't go on like this. We're getting worn down around the edges. We keep running like this, we're gonna slip up. And when we do, we've already gotten a taste of what could happen to us."

Hope kept on driving, looking at the dark and lonely highway in front of her.

"No," Hank said firmly. "No Scott Lang. We do this on our own, our way. It'll be a cold day on the equator before I ask Scott Lang for help again."

It may be freezing before you know it, Hope thought.

<hr />

The first time Hope had encountered Scott wasn't much of an introduction. She didn't even really meet him. She had called the cops on him right after he had broken into Hank's house for the second time.

The next time she met Scott, really met him, was also at Hank's house. Hank had just helped liberate Scott from jail.

"Hello. Who are you?" Scott asked, sitting up in bed. He appeared groggy, confused. It wasn't surprising. He'd used the Ant-Man suit Hank had covertly provided to break out of jail. Then he'd ridden a flying ant to safety. But in the trip from the jail to Pym's house, Scott had blacked out, unfamiliar with the altitude and unique cadence that came with air travel by ant. So when he came to, in a strange bed, in a strange house, with a strange person standing over him, he was a bit nervous.

"Have you been standing there watching me sleep this whole time?" he asked.

Hope didn't say anything. She just stood at the foot of the bed, typing on her phone. After she typed for a while longer, she finally paused.

"Yes," she stated.

"Why?"

It seemed pretty obvious to her why she was watching him. Hope said, "Because the last time you were here you stole something."

"Oh. Oh. Hey, look," Scott said, trying to get out of bed. He was in for a surprise. Scott tried to put a foot on the floor, then glanced down and saw that it was covered in ants. "Whoa!"

"*Paraponera clavata*. Giant tropical bullet ants, ranked highest on the Schmidt Pain Index. They're here to keep an eye on you when I can't," Hope said, nodding sharply at the ants that milled about the floor. "Dr. Pym's waiting for you downstairs," she added, before she turned and left the room.

On her way down the hallway, she heard Scott continuing to talk.

"Who? Hey! Um…Whose pajamas are these?"

Hope couldn't believe what a knucklehead Hank had found.

When she met her father downstairs, he was sitting at the dining room table, reading the paper. He didn't even look up when Hope entered the room. She thought the whole idea of working with Scott Lang to steal the Yellowjacket suit from Darren Cross was a terrible idea. She told him as much.

"I could take down the servers and Cross wouldn't even know it," she said. "We don't need this guy."

That's when Scott walked into the room.

"I assume that you've already met my daughter, Hope," Hank said, still reading the newspaper. He crinkled it a little, then sort of folded it, and set the newspaper on the table.

"I did," Scott said. "She's great."

Hope knew he didn't mean it. But there was still something oddly charming about the way he had said it.

"She doesn't think that we need you," Hank said.

"We don't. We can do this ourselves," Hope protested.

"I go to all this effort to let you steal my suit, then Hope has you arrested," Hank said.

"Okay, we can try this, and when he fails, I'll do it myself," Hope said.

———————●◉●———————

It was still dark as Hope realized she'd been thinking about that first meeting with Scott for a while now. Her father had fallen into a steady sleep in the passenger seat across from her.

She didn't blame her father for being so angry with Scott. Hope felt the same way, and had little or no desire to see him again. Yet, she couldn't help but remember how she had felt about Scott at the very beginning. How she hadn't wanted to give him a chance.

But when she finally had, the guy had proved himself capable of some pretty amazing things.

If only he didn't have to be so...Scott, she thought with a sigh.

CHAPTER TWENTY-TWO

Ant dreams. Scott had them from time to time, ever since he'd woken up that first morning in Hank Pym's house and found the floor covered in ants. He couldn't remember exactly what kind of ants they were, but he remembered something about them causing a lot of pain if they were to sting him.

So, sometimes, he had what he called "ant dreams." They weren't bad or nightmarish or anything like that. They were just...full of ants. Scott would be in the Ant-Man suit, and he would be underground, running. He was always running. And beside him, behind him, all around him, were the ants. And they were running, too, with him.

What were they all running from? Scott was never sure. Before he could ever find out, he always woke up.

So, when he woke up in the middle of the night with a start, Scott thought for sure he had been having another one of his ant dreams. Only when he thought about it for a second, he realized that he had been dreaming about something else. But it felt stronger than a dream. As if it were real. But what was it?

It reminded him of when he had been fighting Darren Cross and gone subatomic to infiltrate the Yellowjacket suit. He kept shrinking and shrinking and shrinking, until he entered what Hank had called the Quantum Realm. Scott couldn't remember anything from his time there, no matter how Hope and Hank had pressed him for information after the fact. It was all a blur.

But this dream he'd just had...Something about it reminded him of how he had felt when he was inside the Quantum Realm. There was a voice, maybe? Someone talking to him. Or was it Scott who'd been talking? He wasn't sure.

But it bothered him. It bothered him enough that he was about to take an unprecedented step.

He rose from the bed, grabbed his cell phone, and walked downstairs. He took in a long, deep breath and stared at the keypad. Just by dialing the number, Scott was opening himself up to a world of trouble. By talking to the person on the other end, he was potentially making his life miserable for the next twenty years.

I need someone to talk me out of this, Scott thought. *Where's Luis? Oh, right, sleeping, like any normal person.*

Then he had an idea. He knew someone who might be awake, someone who could talk him out of making a phone call that could destroy his life. Someone with a daughter who liked to wake up during the night, so naturally her mom had to be a light sleeper. Oh yeah, and she was married to a police officer.

"Maggie?" Scott said as his ex-wife answered the phone.

"Scott? Do you know what time it is?" Maggie said, not sounding groggy at all despite its being the middle of the night. Then: "Is everything all right? Are you okay?"

"Yeah, yeah, I'm fine," Scott said, not believing it. "I had...a pretty weird dream, and it just sort of freaked me out. I guess I just needed to hear a familiar voice, you know?"

"Sure, of course," Maggie said. They had known each other for a long time, and Maggie had an almost instantaneous ability to calm Scott's nerves. "Was the dream about Cassie?"

"No, nothing like that," Scott said. "It was just...I can't put my finger on it, but I think I know someone who could help me sort it out."

"Then why not call them?" Maggie asked.

"It's complicated," Scott said. "First off, I'm not sure they want to hear from me. Second, I'm not sure it's smart of me to do that, given my . . . situation."

"I see," Maggie said slowly. "So, what—are you looking for permission?"

"I'm not looking for permission, Maggie," Scott said. "I want someone to tell me not to call. To tell me I'm just being ridiculous and it was just a dream and I should just go back to sleep."

Without missing half a beat, Maggie replied, "You're being ridiculous, it was just a dream, and you should go back to sleep."

Scott laughed. "Set myself up for that," he said.

Maggie sighed. "You'll do the right thing, Scott. I'd say you always do, but you don't. But I know you'll do what you think is best."

"Thanks, Maggie. Give Cassie a kiss for me, okay?" Scott said, then he hung up the phone.

You're being an idiot, Scott, he thought to himself. *Go back to bed. It was nothing. Just a dream. Be a big boy. Go to sleep.*

When he woke up again, he was sure this time that it wasn't just a dream. Scott was covered in sweat, and he was panting as if he had been running a marathon. He felt jumpy, disconcerted. He had that same feeling again, as if he . . . as if he had actually *been* in the Quantum Realm.

He looked outside and saw the sun was coming up. He wondered how long he would put off making the call.

CHAPTER TWENTY-THREE

I know I shouldn't be doing this.

That's what Scott kept repeating in his head, over and over.

I know I shouldn't be doing this.

But I'm totally going to do it anyway.

He toyed briefly with the idea of sending a text message instead of calling. He tried writing and then rewriting the message. *It's just a text,* he told himself. *All you have to do is hit* SEND, *and then you're done. That way you didn't call anyone. You didn't talk with anybody.*

Just hit SEND, and tell Hope all about the dream.

But he couldn't do it.

Not now. Too much had crossed between them. Maybe someday, maybe when he didn't have the threat of twenty years of jail time hanging over his head, too.

And Hank? *Hank probably thinks I'm an idiot,* Scott thought. *But he always thought I was an idiot. I can live with that.*

So he mustered his courage and dialed Hank Pym's phone number.

It had been a long night, and Hope was tired of driving. She was tired of running. Just plain tired. Of everything.

The buzzing of Hank's phone broke her concentration for a moment.

"Aren't you going to see who it is?" she asked.

"Who do we know would possibly try to contact us?" Hank asked.

Still, he decided to take a look.

When he didn't say anything, Hope knew immediately who it was.

Scott.

Lang.

"You're not going to believe this," Hank said, looking at Hope.

That was either the smartest thing I could have done, Scott thought, *or the stupidest. There's kinda no in between.*

There was no way he could take the voice mail message back. If Agent Woo and the other feds found out about it, it would be Scott's neck for sure. But the only people Scott knew who could possibly help him interpret that dream, and what it might mean, were Hope Van Dyne and Hank Pym.

"I wonder if she's gonna punch me in the face again," Scott said out loud.

All there was left to do now was wait and find out.

EPILOGUE

"Hey, Hank...it's been a while."

The voice belonged to Scott Lang.

"Not sure this number even works anymore. And I know you probably don't want to hear from me anyway, but...Well, I just had a really weird dream."

Hope rolled her eyes.

"Just listen," Hank said, pointing at the phone resting on the table between him and Hope.

"I guess that's not an emergency, except it felt really real. I was back in the Quantum Realm. And...I think I saw your wife."

Hope's eyes went wide, and she stared at her father.

"And there was a little girl. I'm pretty sure it was Hope. Your wife's very pretty, by the way, great hands. Okay, hearing this out loud, definitely not an emergency, sorry I bothered you. I'm sorry for a lot of things."

End of message.

But Hope knew it was also a beginning.

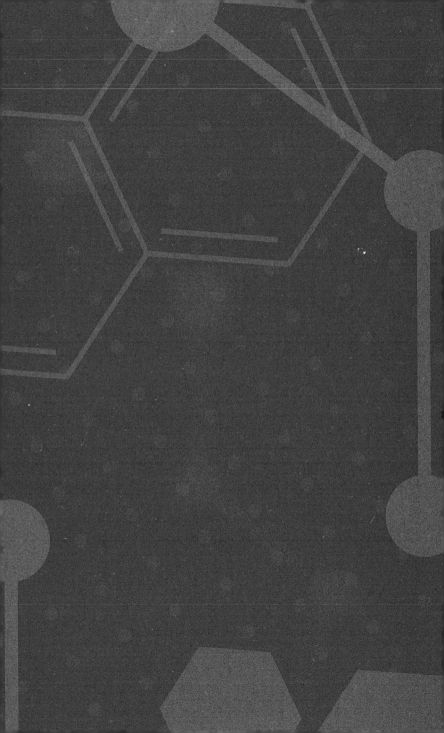

BOOKS FOR THE
ULTIMATE MARVEL FAN

Read these adventures featuring
your favorite Marvel heroes!

Available wherever books are sold

 LITTLE, BROWN AND COMPANY
BOOKS FOR YOUNG READERS   LBYR.com

 © 2018 MARVEL
©2018 CPII

MARVEL

© 2018 MARVEL